Hezekiah Butterworth, H. Winthrop Peirce

The Knight of Liberty

A Tale of the Fortunes of La Fayette

Hezekiah Butterworth, H. Winthrop Peirce

The Knight of Liberty
A Tale of the Fortunes of La Fayette

ISBN/EAN: 9783337088415

Printed in Europe, USA, Canada, Australia, Japan

Cover: Foto ©Andreas Hilbeck / pixelio.de

More available books at **www.hansebooks.com**

"I will take your dispatches to America in person."

THE KNIGHT OF LIBERTY

A Tale of the Fortunes of La Fayette

BY

HEZEKIAH BUTTERWORTH

AUTHOR OF IN OLD NEW ENGLAND, THE PATRIOT SCHOOLMASTER,
THE BOYS OF GREENWAY COURT, IN THE BOYHOOD OF LINCOLN,
THE LOG SCHOOL-HOUSE ON THE COLUMBIA, ETC.

ILLUSTRATED BY H. WINTHROP PEIRCE

NEW YORK
D. APPLETON AND COMPANY
1895

" Where Liberty dwells there ever
will be the country of La Fayette."

PREFACE.

I N each volume of this series the writer has sought to relate some remarkable story associated with the life of a hero in such a way as to picture the history of that hero, making the historical character the background of the narrative. The strange story of Francis K. Huger in this volume is substantially true, and is told to illustrate the life of Lafayette, the Knight of Liberty. Not only is the outline of the narrative true, but, although the book is written in the spirit and after the methods of fiction, nearly all the incidents are historical.

The heroes of these volumes are the creators of American Liberty: Adams, Washington, Lafayette, Lincoln, Marcus Whitman; and a new volume may picture the life of William Penn.

CONTENTS.

LIST OF ILLUSTRATIONS.

THE KNIGHT OF LIBERTY.

CHAPTER I.

THE RESCUE OF LAFAYETTE.

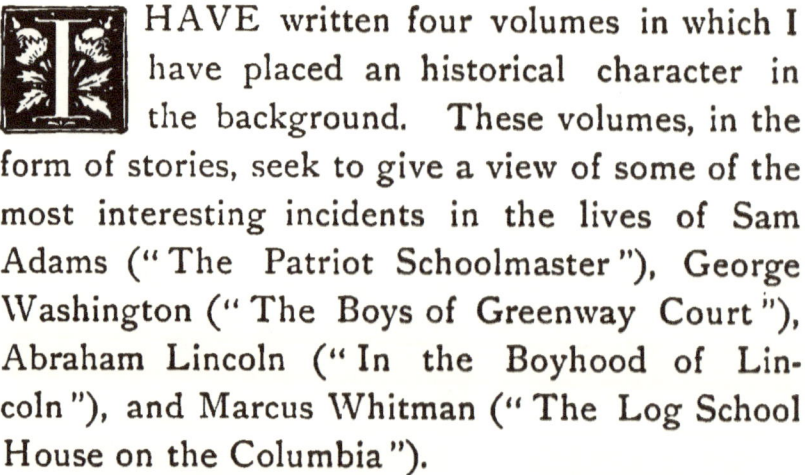 HAVE written four volumes in which I have placed an historical character in the background. These volumes, in the form of stories, seek to give a view of some of the most interesting incidents in the lives of Sam Adams ("The Patriot Schoolmaster"), George Washington ("The Boys of Greenway Court"), Abraham Lincoln ("In the Boyhood of Lincoln"), and Marcus Whitman ("The Log School House on the Columbia").

I am now asked to continue these stories of the most unselfish men in the great events of American history. Every noble man has some strange or remarkable story connected with his life, the telling of which pictures his whole history. Who shall I next take as a representative of what

is most unselfish in American history? William
Penn? Roger Williams among the Indians? Lafayette, the friend of Washington and the apostle
of liberty?

I have chosen Lafayette because he is among
the most unselfish of the world's heroes and benefactors, and because there is one of the most
remarkable stories associated with his history that
I have ever met with in the life of any public man.
It is a story not commonly known ; it is encour-
aging to those who follow the Divine Ought, or
the true spirit within, instead of policy, and I love
to draw upon such material as this.

Lafayette gave himself to mankind, and he
stands for a cause that will live forever. But
unselfish as he was, he had dark days of injustice,
and in those days he found a true friend in
one whose young heart was as unselfish as his
own.

The world treats us exactly as we treat the
world ; our conduct all returns to ourselves, for
like seeks like, and duty done for duty's sake is
sure of its compensations, though they may come
in mysterious and unexpected ways.

But to the strange story I have to tell, the

study of which tends to strengthen one's faith in God and man.

You have read of Lafayette's visits to America, when the very air seemed to ring with his name. Did you know that he suffered for years in dungeons, and that no one but his persecutors and jailers knew where he was? That his disappearance was one of the mysteries of the world? And did you ever hear of two students who went in search of him, like Blondel for King Richard?

I must first introduce you to Lafayette, the young French officer, before these events happened.

CHAPTER II.

HAVE you heard the news from America?"

A gay company of men in glittering uniforms started, and sat in a listening attitude.

"I see you have not. The colonies have united, and declared their independence of the Crown in the name of Liberty. Was there ever audacity like that! One Jefferson is leading the movement. It means war. Authority against Liberty, and the end of it all is not hard to see. The discontent should have been crushed out long ago, but at last the king is aroused, and he will put down rebellion there with a firm hand."

The speaker was the Duke of Gloucester, brother of George III. The place, a military banquet hall, at the great German fortress of Metz. Afar the Moselle lay gleaming, and the parks and gardens around the ponderous fortifi-

4

cations were glowing with fresh leaves and flowers.

"What do the American colonies want of liberty? Why should they resist being taxed for a good government which they know not how to administer themselves! They claim that all men are born free and equal, and that the sense of the majority should rule. Why, such an idea would overturn the whole wisdom of the past. And to what an extent have they gone! They would make their public officers the servants of the people. Think of that! They would elect officers to be the servants of the people, and call such a government as that Liberty! And furthermore they declare that the liberty to do right is the birthright of every man! Who would want to live in a land like that?"

"I would!"

The speaker was a young French officer in his nineteenth year. He had been listening to the words of the duke. His face flashed and glowed, and his hand trembled on the hilt of his sword. The word "Liberty" seemed to thrill him. From a boy he had had an inward conviction that he was born to be a defender of Liberty, and

2

leader of the cause of human freedom in the world. That young man was the Marquis de La-fayette.

"What are the dispatches that you have received from America?" asked an English officer of the duke.

"That the colonies are in rebellion. That the Colonists are about to maintain their belief in the equal rights of man."

"I would gladly draw my sword in such a cause as that," said the young Marquis de Lafayette to a friend in a low voice. "I am assured that some such cause is to be my destiny. There are times when the soul hears a voice that calls it to duty and makes that duty clear. The voice comes as it were from the heavens. The soul which has been haunted by ideals and made rest-less hears it and owns it, and makes it the captain of its life. The duke's words have a strange meaning to me. I myself believe in the liberty of men to do right, and I do not believe in the right of Crowns to compel men to do wrong."

The duke was about to speak.

"The colonists hold that governments are instituted for the good of the people. Could such an idea triumph, it would reverse the order of the world."

The American idea and purpose thrilled the heart of the young marquis. The duke, in condemning the American people had expressed his own views in those of the colonists.

"I believe in that cause," said Lafayette to a brother officer. "I believe in it with all my heart. I hold to the equal rights and brotherhood of all mankind. Call it what you will, every man should have the right to do right and should never be compelled to do wrong. I care not for fame, nor power, nor wealth, for their own sake; I would gladly draw my sword, and give my fortune to a cause like that, even if it brought me poverty and loss. I would like to espouse the cause of the colonists."

"But your young wife?" said the officer, checking his friend's ardent aspirations.

The young marquis answered—we follow the thoughts of his early inspirations as related in later years: "No private affection can ever divert me from public duty. I have a bride whom I love with a devotion as great as any living man. But if

I were to draw my sword in the name of Liberty
she would one day be proud that I had done so.
What is the use of life but to live for the things
that live, and for the highest cause that can
claim our service? What is selfish pleasure like
suffering for a cause? I must be what I ought
to be. But hold, listen! what is the duke
saying?"

"Our forces have routed the Americans at
Bunker Hill, but they have left Boston, and the
struggle now goes on in New York and New
Jersey."

"Boston!" It may have been the first time that
the marquis ever heard that word as applied to an
American town. Lafayette had been born at the
Château Chavagnac, Auvergne, France, September 6, 1757. His father, a brave French officer,
had fallen at Minden, and his mother had died in
1770, leaving a great fortune and vast estates.
He inherited from his parents a love of liberty
that was the ruling passion of his soul. His boyhood had been unlike other boys'. It had been a
dream of the welfare of humanity. He had early
entered the army and was stationed at Metz when
the English duke arrived, and he had been

included among the guests at this memorable
banquet—a banquet in which the destiny of
America seems to have been determined, for the
inspiration that day in the soul of Lafayette led
to final triumphs of the American armies at Yorktown.

"And who," said Lafayette, rising, "is the
leader of the American army?"

He listened.

"GEORGE WASHINGTON," said an English officer,
bowing across the glittering board.

"George Washington!" Had the Marquis de
Lafayette ever heard that name before! We
know not. It was a name of destiny to him now.
Washington, the father of liberty! His mission
leaped into his mind in full force. The freedom
of the American colonies should be his grand purpose in life, and he would unite his sword with
that of the unknown leader of liberty in the
West.

The banquet ended. The summer night came
on over the Moselle and its old towers and bloom-
ing gardens. But young Lafayette's thoughts
were with the colonies struggling for freedom in
the West.

He sought the Duke of Gloucester, and the two talked together long on the purpose of the English colonies. "We must crush the colonies," said the duke. "They are in rebellion. It will be an easy thing to do. Authority must be respected."

"And crush liberty—the liberty of the new world," thought the young marquis.

The Moselle darkened; the stars came out, and the young marquis wandered out on the esplanade.

" Washington—George Washington !"

That banquet had made him one of the most unselfish heroes of liberty who ever drew the sword. But how should he find the field of struggle, more than three thousand miles away? He dreamed that night under the moon and stars, and his dream came true.

"Every man is a debtor to his calling," he thought. "I must be that which I ought to be or else I shall be nothing. Nobler deeds than man has ever done remain to be done. Liberty, I would find thy field. I was born for thee! Where? How?"

Such, as we gather from his memoirs, must

have been the dreams of Lafayette at this time. Destiny had shown him her face, like Selene to Endymion in the fable. He knew for what he was born, but again and again came the question—"How shall I find the field?"

CHAPTER III.

THERE was an American commissioner in Paris. His name was Silas Deane. He was born at Groton, Conn., 1737, and graduated at Yale College, 1758. He had been a member of the Continental Congress in 1774, and had been sent to France as the financial agent of the united Colonies.

Young Lafayette left Metz to consult with this man.

"I have come," said Lafayette, "to offer my sword to the liberties of your country. I hope that your cause is advancing. It is one of the noblest in the world."

"No," said Mr. Deane, "if the dispatches that have just arrived are true, the cause is not advancing. The news is that the 'insurgents,' as the patriots are called, have been driven toward Philadelphia, through the Jerseys, by a powerful force of British regulars. The news may not be

trustworthy, but it has prevented me from secur-
ing credit for America. My friend Benjamin
Franklin will soon be here, and I will present you
to him, and you may trust his advice and sound-
ness of judgment. You are a rich man, I
believe."

"I have an ample fortune."

His income from his estates was some $37,000
per year.

"More than ample for my own wants, and in
espousing the cause of America I seek not to add
to my fortune, but to spend what I can spare in
this crisis of human need. I have no thought of
going to America for pay. All that I have and
am I offer to the cause of liberty, which is not of
America alone, but of all mankind. I feel within
myself a calling to which I must be true."

Silas Deane saw in Lafayette one of these
young men who become powerful by giving up
self for the service of others. He introduced him
to Benjamin Franklin, who also saw in the young
marquis a soul that at once won his admiration. Franklin was one of the American commissioners.

The commissioners agreed to consider this offer

"When," says Lafayette, in his memoirs, "I presented my boyish face to Mr. Deane, I spoke more of my ardor in the cause than of my experience. But I dwelt upon the effect that my departure would excite in France, and he signed my documents."

One loves to picture that "boyish face."

So young Lafayette gave his name, fame, and influence to the cause of freedom in a foreign land, as a debtor to his inward calling. He went·to Passy, where Dr. Franklin was, and there he met a German officer, as patriotic as himself, Baron de Kalb. This officer, too, had espoused the cause of liberty, believing it to be the cause of the world. He was older than Lafayette, having been born in Bavaria, 1721. The two became friends. They thought they had secured a ship at Bordeaux, but the ship could not at once be got ready for sea. So they with other volunteers to the American cause, hurried to Passage, a Spanish port, to engage another conveyance.

But Lafayette's patriotism was to be still further put to the test.

At Bordeaux there came to him an order from the king of the French :.

"You must not leave the country. Repair to Marseilles."

Should he disobey the king? Should he imperil his estates and his fortune? Should he endanger his noble wife?

"Thou must be that which thou oughtest to be," said the spirit of his calling. Yes, for liberty.

"What will you do?" asked his brother volunteers. "Will you return?"

"No—I must go! And you?"

"We will go!"

They were words of fate. Lafayette went to Marseilles, but returned again. So out of the Spanish port he and his eleven comrades sailed, leaving all things but honor, to give their swords to the cause of liberty in the West.

There is no nobler page of history than this, and nothing more worthy may tempt historic fiction.

On the sea, in peril of capture, with nothing to hope for but the victory of liberty! On, on, to the coasts of the Carolinas, where the patriots arrived in June, 1777.

"The moment I heard of America I loved her. The moment I knew she was fighting for liberty I burned with desire to bleed for her."

So said Lafayette in a letter to the President
of the Continental Congress.

He was now in America, the land of his dreams,
and he was only about twenty years of age.

On landing, a very notable incident occurred.
The shores of the New World filled the two officers, Lafayette and Baron de Kalb, with an
inspirational feeling. Their emotions impelled
them to make their vows to God. The doors of
heaven might open to hear it, for nobler men
never breathed forth their purpose in life.

Above them glowed the summer sky of the
Carolinas. It was night as the two stood upon
the shore.

"I pledge myself and all that I have to the
cause of the liberty of America," said Lafayette,
"and I offer my life to this sacred cause."

"America, I pledge myself and all that I am to
thee and the cause of human freedom!" said
Baron de Kalb.

The incident is a true one—the stars were
above them, and behind them rolled the sea.
Such in substance were the vows of these two
men, as they landed in America.

They saw a light in the distance. They went

toward it. It was in the plantation house of Major Benjamin Huger.

Morning showed a landscape blossoming with magnolias; in the sunny plantations the mocking-birds were singing, and the two officers here first saw the sun of the New World. Were those midnight resolutions sentiments? If so, they were sentiments that made character, and character destiny, and that helped give to mankind its birthright, to toiling millions a field of labor, and the rights of labor their dues. The birthrights of universal liberty were in them.

CHAPTER IV.

LAFAYETTE MEETS A BRIGHT BOY.

T the house of Major Huger a strange incident happened. Major Huger had a son, who was destined to become in future years "the deliverer of Lafayette." His name was Francis K. Huger. His portrait in a frame of gold once hung, and may now probably be seen, at Lagrange, the château of Lafayette. It bears this inscription :

FRANCIS K. HUGER.
Presented to
GENERAL LAFAYETTE,
by the City of Charleston,
through
Samuel Prioleau,
Intendant,
1825.
Made by Fletcher and Gardnier, Phil.

The portrait represents a man of broad forehead with width of ideality, of a refined, slender face, a prominent nose, and thin, resolute lips.

People walk slowly before it and say that that picture represents "The Deliverer of Lafayette." The Carolinas have always been proud of this young man and his heroic deed. His name is pronounced *Huzay* or *Huzhay*.

Lafayette loved children, and this boy, Francis, soon found himself in the patriot's lap, and we, with a questioning curiosity, may fancy his inquiries to have been something like these:

"You have come over the sea?"

"Yes, my boy, a far, far journey."

"But, please sir, why did you come?"

"To help the people gain their liberties."

"But, please sir, you have your liberty."

"Yes, my boy, in a measure. I could have more."

"And you sailed over the sea to help us?"

"Yes, we hope to help your country."

"Please sir, will they pay you?"

"Yes, my boy."

"Who?"

"Everybody, my heart here—heaven—you; perhaps you will one day pay me."

"You came because you loved us?"

"Yes, my boy."

3

"One day we will all love you. I do now."

"And I love you, my boy."

"Shall we ever meet again? I mean after you go away?"

Lafayette looked into the beautiful eyes of the little Southerner.

"I do not know what may be in store for us. Love never dies."

"I shall love you always. And if I grow up, I will pay you."

"What a heart you have, my boy!"

"You love people whom you have never seen?"

"Yes."

"Perhaps people whom you have never seen will love you some day."

"Yes, that is the way that things happen, my boy; whatever may befall me, I do not believe I will ever be entirely forsaken, for those who help others always find help in their needs."

"Please sir, are you a rich man? I hope so."

"Yes, I have a good fortune."

"Then you will never want."

"I cannot tell. People who have fortunes are sometimes forsaken. It is the heart of love that does not forsake one in misfortune."

Lafayette and his future deliverer.

"Suppose you were to lose your fortune, and be poor, and all folks forget you, or lose you, please sir, what would you do?"

"I would trust. Some heart would find me. The world treats us as we treat the world. Some true heart would find me."

The boy and the young officer became friends. It was a link in the chain of destiny.

CHAPTER V.

AFAYETTE furnished money to Charleston to provide clothing for the soldiers under General Moultrie, and he and Baron de Kalb started in a carriage for Philadelphia, where the Continental Congress was, late in June, 1777.

It was the fall tide of the year. The plantations were green with vegetation and gay with bloom. The fame of the officers had preceded them, and caused the patriots in some places to await their coming. The roads were in parts of the country new, and all things were novel to the two officers and their friends.

They rode rapidly.

"We must make a short journey," said they. "It is a ride for liberty!"

The distance was some seven hundred miles. The coach rolled forward as if it were for a re-enforcement. The party stopped to cool in the

24

shadows of mountains, and beside sunny-bosomed
waters. They rested a little at inns and plantation houses, but they were impatient to meet the
American patriotic leaders, and Washington and
the army of liberty.

In the rapid ride the coach broke down.

" Horses are better than coaches," said they,
and they left the coach, and hurried forward on
horseback, riding with the utmost speed.

Through the burning Carolinas, through Virginia, across the Potomac, where the glorious
dome of the Capitol and the Washington monument would in the coming century rise in air,
they pursued their way.

Did a stranger ask the cause of their haste?

" We are riding for liberty ! "

Did he ask who they were hurrying so impetu-
ously to see ?

" Washington and the army of liberty ! "

The patriots who knew them cheered them as
they passed. The British minister in Paris had
tried to prevent them from coming to America,
and their flight had created a great impression
in Europe, and their arrival was destined to
be an inspiration here. They came flying into

Philadelphia, met the patriotic leaders, and one of the first acts of Lafayette was to present to Washington sixty thousand francs, to meet a crisis of the cause.

Lafayette offered to enter the army as a common soldier. Washington read his soul when they first met, and soon secured for him a major general's commission.

Fate, fortune, Providence, rode with them on those midsummer days through the Carolinas and Virginia ; over the hills of Maryland and Pennsylvania ; past the Southern cotton fields, and Northern fields of corn. The young Frenchman was bearing victory with him. He saw the future and his soul glowed. He bore in his young heart the inspiration of the ages. The cause of the liberty of the world was in that ride ! It was one of the grandest rides in history, to which Charles Sumner paid the tribute of some of the best passages of a grand oration.

CHAPTER VI.

THE WHITE COCKADE.

MAJOR BENJAMIN HUGER, at whose plantation house little Francis Kinlock Huger had first met Lafayette, was one of the five patriot brothers, who were farmers in the Carolinas. This man was killed by an accident before his own lines in Charleston, 1779.

One autumn day, not many months after this event, there came riding down to the Huger plantation an orderly of William Augustine Washington, a kinsman of George Washington. This orderly reined his steed before the door of the patriot's mansion.

The family hurried out to give a welcome and to inquire the news. The orderly seemed in high spirits and pointed to his hat. On his hat was a white rosette on a ground of black.

" Has there been a victory?" asked one of the family.

" Yes, good friends, something more than vic-

tory. Our independence is now as sure as any
event can be."

He pointed again to the rosette.

"What has happened?" broke from all lips.

"Lafayette!"

He was bidden to dismount, and he entered the
house gayly, and a meal was prepared for him.

The little boy again seemed all eyes and ears.
He climbed upon the stranger's knees as he had
done on Lafayette's when the latter came up
from the seaside after pledging his all, under the
night sky, to the independence of America.

"Did Lafayette give you the white rose on
your hat?" asked the boy.

"No; Washington."

"William Washington, was it, sir?"

"No, General George Washington."

"What did he give you the ribbon for, sir?"

"For a cockade."

"What is a cockade, sir?"

"It is a rosette to wear on the hat. General
George Washington has ordered that all the officers of the army shall wear white rosettes on their
hats, in honor of the return of Lafayette."

"Lafayette, Lafayette!" said the boy, "I was

the first one that he ever kissed in America. He
said that he loved America when he first heard
her name spoken ; and then he said he loved me,
and he held me in his lap just as you do now and
he let me ask him questions. Where has Lafayette been, sir ? You said he had returned."

"He has been to France, my little boy, for I
must tell the story through you, and well I may,
as you were among the first to welcome him.
He has been to France to secure a French army
from the king to give us independence, and he
has done it. He has landed at Newport with an
army and navy, under the great Count Rochambeau !"

"Then the vow to win liberty for America that
he made out there on the coast by the sea was an
honest one. Look out yonder—there is where he
was, sir !"

A wide vista opened through the magnolias,
and afar lay the cotton fields and beyond them
rolled the sea.

"He saw a light," said the boy.

"When he landed ?" asked the orderly.

"Yes; it was ours; I am glad it was ours.
Who would have thought that he would have met

me, *me?* I wonder if I will ever see him again! He put his arms around me, so. Of all the great men in the world, next to Washington, I would rather see Lafayette."

"We have let the boy talk long enough," said a brother of Major Huger. "You have good news to tell. Let us have it. Francis, you will be quiet now while the orderly tells us the news."

"Lafayette left Boston in February [1779] and, after a short winter voyage arrived at Brest. The French court received him with favor, though the king was obliged to imprison him for one week for leaving the country contrary to his orders. The imprisonment only amused the court and his prison was but a room in his brother-in-law's house. When his punishment was over, all Paris hailed him with delight and honor. The king listened to his plea for America as to a son, and granted him a powerful fleet, and an army six thousand strong."

"Glory to Lafayette!" exclaimed the boy, "Glory—look out there—he promised all this to us out *there!*"

"Be quiet, my little friend," said the orderly.

"Be quiet! how could I be quiet? I would like to crow."

"Well, not now. The French fleet and army arrived at Newport July 10 [1780]. Bells rung, and flags are flying in all the East. We must put flags all over the plantation houses. By the way, have you heard of the boast that General Tarleton has made?"

"No; he is the most brutal officer that has ever appeared on the field. What is his threat?" said one of the family.

"He says that he will send William Washington to London in chains; that he will put the British flag over every plantation house in the Carolinas, and that he will drink his victory out of Lady Ashe's punch bowl."

"What is Lady Ashe's punch bowl?" asked the boy.

"Oh, it is a famous bowl in Wilmington, or in some of the houses belonging to the great family."

"But he will have to get William Washington before he can send him to London in chains, will he not?"

"Yes, my boy. And he will have to subdue the Carolinas more than he has yet, to put the

British flag over every plantation house. As for the Albemarle punch bowl, I will tell you the story of that after dinner. But I have not told you all the news yet."

The family listened intently.

"The King of France has made General George Washington lieutenant general of the empire of France, so that he may outrank the French general who has come to America."

"Glory to the king!" said the boy. "What color does he wear?"

"White, my son; Bourbon lilies."

"What is that?" said the orderly, pointing to his hat.

"You said it was a cockade."

"What color is it?"

"White."

"It did not use to be white."

"The one that father used to wear was black. What changed it to white?"

"The order of Washington, as I said, in honor of Lafayette. All the American officers are henceforth to wear the white cockade."

The boy looked wistfully at the orderly's hat.

"I wish you would give it to me."

" What, my hat ? "

" No ; the white cockade."

" You shall have it, my boy, for I have another. You ought to have one, as you were among the first to welcome Lafayette."

The orderly gave the boy the rosette. Francis placed it on his own hat, and walked to and fro, to the delight of the family. He saluted each one, lifting his right hand.

" I wish that *he* could see me now," said he.

" Who see you ? " asked the orderly.

" General Lafayette ! "

CHAPTER VII.

THE ALBEMARLE PUNCH BOWL.

THE orderly was called to a sumptuous dinner, after which the family again gathered around him, and the boy asked for the story of Lady Ashe's punch bowl, for the way that the officer had alluded to it had much excited his curiosity.

"The Albemarle punch bowl," he said; "you have heard of it, no doubt. It has a long history, but I am not going to tell that, my boy. It never will be mended again; there were pieces enough to have decorated a regiment. Lady Ashe made thorough work of it."

"Is it broken?" asked Mrs. Huger.

"Broken? yes, it has been dashed into a hundred pieces."

"It was the pride of the family," said Mrs. Huger, "and many a time has it served them in the old banquet halls. Did the British officers destroy it?"

34

"No. Lady Ashe did it with her own hands. You have heard," he continued, with the boy at his knee, "that General Tarleton once boasted that he would send William Washington to London in chains; that he would put the British flag over every plantation house in the Carolinas, and would drink his victory out of Lady Ashe's punch bowl. You know what the family of General Ashe are. They stand by the honor of the general, who was the soul of the old Provincial Congress, and who raised a regiment at his own expense, even though he was defeated at Briar Creek. The British have never ceased to annoy his family since Wilmington fell into their hands. Now, this is the queer story that the people are telling: Lady Ashe is a woman of mettle, and I think it may be true. When she heard of General Tarleton's boast, she said to an American:

"'I will see—General Tarleton dines at your house to-morrow, I believe.'

"'Yes, would you like to meet him?' asked the gentleman.

"'I would like to speak to him on the occasion,' said the lady.

"'Then you will be my guest.'

" The day came. General Tarleton and his
staff were present at the fine old house, and Lady
Ashe was among the guests.

" ' I would like to meet your Colonel Washington,' said General Tarleton. ' I have never seen
him.'

" ' If you had only looked behind you, after the
battle of Cowpens, you might have done so,' said
Lady Ashe.

" It was a sharp retort to remind Tarleton of his
retreat then and there in the guest rooms. But
Lady Ashe never feared the face of day.

" The tables were spread, and the British officers
assembled, feeling that they were doing honor to
by their host their presence. Wine began to flow,
when one of the guests said :

" ' Lady Ashe, now is the time for the Albemarle punch bowl.'

" ' Wait a few minutes,' said she ; 'and I will
bring it.'

" She arose and left the room.

" The guests waited.

" Presently the door was opened. Lady Ashe
came into the room slowly and with a radiant face.
She held the punch bowl over her head. It was

brimming with roses. The flowers filled the room with fragrance. Were they swimming on a sur-face of waving punch?

"She came forward with measured step, as if to a minuet, casting her eyes at times up to the great pile of roses above her. When she had reached the head of the table she stopped, and stood like a statue, with uplifted eyes.

"How beautiful and noble and regal she looked!

"The guests were astonished and silent. No one moved. She did not lower the great bowl. At last, amid the deep silence she dropped her eyes on the guests, and then fixed them on the British officer.

"'General Tarleton,' she said, in a deep, musical voice; 'General Tarleton, this is the Albemarle punch bowl. Many members of the Provincial Congress have admired it for its beauty, and it has found a place in many gatherings of patriots, though they were not drinking men. Men with a purpose do not dine and wine much, but this bowl, as a work of beauty and art, has been the pride of our family treasures. It is not filled with punch to-day; it is filled with roses.

4

"'General Tarleton, look at it. Why is it filled with roses, instead of punch? Because we are poor? No, we have fallen under your power, but we are not poor. Because we are inhospitable? Carolinians would be hospitable, though poor.

"'General Tarleton, listen. I hear that you have grown boastful of late. I hear that you have said that you would send William Washington to London in chains, and would put the British flag over every plantation house in the Carolinas. Is that so, General Tarleton?'

"'I will send William Washington to London in chains, if I can get him, madam; and I would be glad, madam, to see my own flag flying over all the plantation houses in the Carolinas, as they are floating here to-day.'

"'And, General Tarleton, I hear that you have also boasted that you will celebrate your victory by the use of this punch bowl.

"'General Tarleton——'

"Lady Ashe dashed the punch bowl to the floor, breaking it into a thousand pieces.

"'General Tarleton, that is one part of your prophecy that will never be fulfilled!'

"I hope the story is true; if it be not, it

ought to be, and reports do not spring out of the earth."

"Lafayette will drive the British from Wilmington, will he not?" asked the boy.

"So I hope. He is, I hear, given in part the direction of the Southern campaign," said the orderly.

"Lafayette shall be my hero, after Washington," said the boy, "and I will never surrender the white cockade."

The boy touched his hat, and the company laughed, and the orderly said:

"Good, my boy; Lafayette shall be your hero and a hero of that hero may you ever be proud to be!"

Later in the day, little Francis Huger had the orderly to himself. He may have recalled the unusual attention that he had received from Lafayette. Be that as it may, his fancy was excited, and his thoughts were inquisitive, though nobly so.

"Orderly John," he said, for so the popular orderly and courier was called, "what if Lafayette should help us gain our liberties; would he then not be a great man like Washington?"

"He certainly would, my boy."

"Orderly John, suppose he then should go back, and sometime return to this country again. Would not all the people be glad?"

"Yes."

"And shout?"

"Yes."

"So would I. Do you suppose that he would remember me?"

"I think that he would."

"Why?"

"He met you at a great crisis of his life."

"What do you mean by crisis?"

"He had just made a vow, as you know; he saw the light of your house; he was lonely, and he turned his heart to you. He could never forget it."

"I wish I could do something to honor him, Orderly John. What is the greatest thing a man could do for another man, Orderly John?"

"To be willing to lay down his life for him."

"I would never have such a chance, would I?"

"I cannot tell. This world brings many changes. Events come to those who have the spirit of them."

"What do you mean by that, Orderly John?"

"The things that we would do sometimes come to us."

"Orderly John, *that* would be the happiest hour in my life. What thing of all the world would make a man like Lafayette most happy?"

"I think, my boy, that the thing that would make a hero most happy would be the triumph of his cause."

"Yes, and what else."

"Well, to meet an unknown man who had offered to give up his life for him."

"To meet an unknown man who had offered to give up his life for him? Why would that make him so happy, Orderly John?"

"He would then meet one who had loved him better than himself. There could be no other meeting like that."

"This nation may be free, and Lafayette may go away; and it may grow, and invite him to come back again. I like to dream of it, and, Orderly John, I like to dream that when that day comes, I will be there. I like to fancy such things. Do dreams come true?"

"Yes, often, my boy. Everyone dreams of

what he would like most to be. Almost every
little boy is a Shakespere in his dreams."

"Oh, Orderly John! I never dream of that.
But everyone can be a kind of Reward of Merit
to others, can he not?"

Lafayette had dreamed his dream of liberty on
the green Carolinian shore. It was coming true,
for he had made a vow of it, and his life was following the grand resolution. Here was a little
dreamer, whose heart was following the fortunes
of Lafayette. Would his dreams one day prove
true?

Desires have eyes, and hopes are events. Are
the boy and the general to meet again? When?
Where? That is our story.

CHAPTER VIII.

" CORNWALLIS IS TAKEN !"

LAFAYETTE was made the principal general of the campaign against Lord Cornwallis, and his movements in Virginia were regarded as among the most brilliant in military history. He compelled the British army to concentrate at a point where they could be seized.

The siege of Yorktown crowned the efforts of Lafayette for American independence. The allied armies joined Lafayette for this last campaign of the revolution, September 25, 1781. The besieging army consisted of sixteen thousand men, under the chief command of Washington, assisted by Rochambeau ; but Lafayette, who had been the directing mind and energy of the environment of the army of Cornwallis, was allowed to consummate his own plan. On September 28 twelve thousand men marched from Williamsburg, driving the British before them into the intrenchments of Yorktown. The allies surrounded the place. The fleet of De Grasse lay off the town in Lynn Haven Bay to prevent any relief of the British troops.

On the night of October 6 the cannonade began from the French ships, and the American army advanced their intrenchments. Day by day the circle of the besieging army contracted around the place. Two British redoubts were carried, and the situation of Lord Cornwallis became most critical.

He resolved to escape by taking his army across the river. Boats were prepared, and the troops began their secret march when a furious storm arose, and the troops returned. The earl now lost all hope, and was forced to sign terms of capitulation.

Lafayette's heart was filled with a patriotic glow when he found that he was forcing Lord Cornwallis into these limits, which must end in capture. Would you know how he felt? The following extract from a letter which he wrote to Washington will picture his soul :

" In the present state of affairs I hope you will come yourself to Virginia. Lord Cornwallis must be attacked with pretty great apparatus; but when the French fleet takes possession of the bay and rivers, and we form a land force superior to his, that army must sooner or later be forced to surrender, as we may get what re-enforcements we please.

"I heartily thank you for having ordered me to remain in Virginia; it is to your goodness that I am indebted *for the most beautiful prospect which I may ever behold.*"

That prospect was realized when Yorktown fell and liberty was won, at that time for America and ultimately for the world.

Lafayette became the hero of two worlds, but it is probable that the surrender of Lord Cornwallis, and the triumph of the American army, was the most beautiful vision that he ever beheld. He fought for the cause of liberty universal, and it was at Yorktown that that cause was won. He must have ever looked upon it as Freedom's coronation day.

"I loved America when I first heard her name," he once said, and which remark we have already quoted. America now was to love his name, forever more, and to honor it with undying fame. He had fulfilled the trust born in his soul.

At midnight, October 23, 1781, an aid-de-camp of Washington rode into Philadelphia from York-town. The watchman had been pacing the streets, crying :

" Past ten o'clock and all is well."

" Past eleven o'clock and all is well."

" Past twelve o'clock and all is well."

The aid-de-camp, Lieutenant Colonel Tilghman, rode up to the house of the President of the Congress and knocked.

" I arrest you," said a watchman. " Why do you disturb the peace ? "

" *Cornwallis is taken !* " said the aid.

" Past one o'clock and Cornwallis is taken !" cried the watchman.

The people heard. Lights flashed from window to window. The old State house bell began to clang.

" Past two o'clock and Cornwallis is taken !" we may fancy the intelligence to have been announced with the hours.

The morning broke amid the booming of cannon. Yorktown had surrendered and the York-

town siege had been the grand campaign of
Lafayette.

Into South Carolina couriers were riding.
Among them was the orderly. He rode out of
his way to the Huger mansion. The family had
seen him and were awaiting him.

"Liberty is won," said the orderly; "Yorktown
has surrendered! Seven thousand men and more
than two hundred cannon! Shout, the world is
taken! Mankind is to be free! Shout! Shout!
The campaign of Lafayette has crowned the
American army; it was Lafayette whose strategy
shut up Cornwallis, and compelled him to surrender his army to Washington! Shout! Shout!
Boy, where is your white cockade?"

"Here, sir."

"Aye, and be true to it ever."

"Lafayette is my hero, sir."

"And the world's. For in fighting for our
liberties he has fought for the freedom of all mankind. The victors at Yorktown will one day
make France itself free. Long live Washington,
and long live Lafayette!"

"What will Lafayette now do?" asked the boy.

"He will return to France, and try to secure

for her people that which he has helped us to win."

This was the history of Lafayette after the American revolution. He went to his beautiful home among the mountains, but the people of France were beginning to struggle to be free.

We must follow Lafayette in these struggles, which made him the hero of the liberties of France. The French republic of to-day owes her glory largely to the character of Lafayette. But Liberty in France was often overthrown before she found her stable place. The leader of progress usually falls a martyr to his cause. But he will not lose faith, if the cause but go on.

CHAPTER IX.

THE WHITE COCKADE OF THE CONSTITUTION.

IN the early struggles of the French for liberty, Lafayette, in whose honor the white cockade had been brought into use in America, became again the hero of the white cockade.

We must tell you how Lafayette came to give to France the white cockade. There was formed a legislative body in France, to make a constitution which should protect the rights of the people, which was called the Constituent Assembly. The king secretly was opposed to this assembly, and began to concentrate an army to sustain his original power. This threw the city of Paris into wild excitement, for the people had resolved in their hearts to be free, and to have a constitution that would protect them in their freedom. Lafayette was a member of this Assembly.

The Assembly asked the king to withdraw his troops from Paris. The king replied by recom-

mending the Assembly to remove from Paris to
some city where soldiers would not be needed.

To do this would be to abandon the cause.
Now came forward Lafayette. " Make a declaration of the rights of man," he said, " as a preamble
to the constitution."

The Assembly resolved to form a National
Guard for its own protection, and that of the constitution which they were forming, and to put at
its head General Lafayette. It was thus that
Lafayette was made the defender of the constitution of France. The king and court were at this
time at Versailles.

The court was at war against the representatives of the people. The excitement in Paris
grew.

It was the 11th of July, 1789. The king still
controlled the army, and Paris believed itself to be
threatened with invasion. In the hot afternoon of
that day a vast crowd assembled at the Palace
Royal.

About three o'clock a young man mounted
a table in the gardens of the Palace and waved
aloft a pistol.

" Citizens !" he cried, " the court is preparing

for us a St. Bartholomew for patriots. Citizens, to arms, to arms ! Let us take the *green* cockade."

That man was a young Picardian, Camille Desmoulins. The people mounted the green ribbon, and those who could not get green ribbons stripped the green leaves from the trees and put them in their hats. The people were resolved to sustain the Assembly ; there should be no surprise —no St. Bartholomew for liberty. So everywhere was seen the green cockade.

The king's soldiers menaced the people, and day by day the excitement grew. The people rushed in great bodies to the armories, demanding arms. They must arm themselves, for as yet the National Guard was not organized. They formed a committee, and this committee resolved to form a militia of forty thousand men. The colors of Paris were blue and red.

"The militia must wear the colors of Paris," said the committee. So the green cockade of the night of the 11th vanished, and the blue and red cockade filled the streets of Paris. The people were arming. The committee ordered the construction of fifty thousand pikes ; they were finished within thirty-six hours. The Intendant of Paris had caused the national arms to be hidden in the cellars of the house of the Invalides.

The sun of the 14th of July rose red and warm.

"On to the Invalides!" began to cry the people, and to the Invalides rushed the heroes of the blue and red cockades. They forced open the doors, and carried away twenty-two thousand guns. The people were now armed. The eventful day blazed, and the ardor for liberty grew.

There was a great prison in Paris called the Bastille. It had been used by a long line of kings to overawe the people. The most cruel courts had caused their enemies to be sent there to rot in dungeons. Wicked men and women, favorites of courts, had been able to send there the most worthy and noble people. It had been the stronghold of injustice, tyranny, and cruelty, for centuries. The people had hated it; all patriotic and good hearts had cried out against it; and now at last the tempest clouds of indignation were gathering around it.

"On to the Bastille!" cried the armed people. So the blue and red cockades. The tempest was gathering force.

They approached the great fortress—the emblem of tyranny—its thick walls and high towers frowning over them. The stoutest fortress is weak if it have a weak heart. The people demanded the surrender of the Bastille. They were fired by a long sense of injustice, which as a rule ends at last in revolt, and they rushed over the drawbridge. The soldiers of the Bastille fired upon them; but the sight of blood only added to the fury of this new army of liberty.

The French garrison within hesitated to fire upon their own people, and demanded of the Governor the surrender of the fortress. The Governor was a tyrant, and all tyrants are cowards, and finding himself beset with enemies within the fortress as well as without, he determined to destroy the fortress and end his own life.

He descended to the powder magazine to apply the torch to the powder, and thus blow up the fortress, his own soldiers, and the enemy. There were thirty-five casks of powder in the magazine, and a spark there would have made one of the most awful slaughters of history. Suddenly there stepped across his way two French guards.

5

"Halt!" They placed before him two bayonets.

"Capitulate!"

The governor, with his crimes of years, shrunk back. Could the Bastille be so easily taken? Yes, wrong falls easily, at a breeze, when it is fully ripe. The terror-stricken man promised to capitulate, and was led away.

The besiegers were victorious. They lowered the bridge that led to the fortress. The people came pouring into the fortress. What a sight was revealed! What loathsome dungeons! What skeletons of prisoners!

They released the prisoners, and as they saw what the Bastille was their fury grew. They began to tear down the fortress with their own hands. They felt their strength and knew that the fall of the Bastille was the end of the one man power in France. They slew the governor, and placed his head on a pike.

The sunset of the 14th of July was the end of the arbitrary French monarchy. The Constitution was to rise, defended by the National Guard.

At midnight a messenger entered the apartments of the king.

" Is it a revolt?" asked the king.

"Sire, it is a revolution."

On the 15th of July Paris rang with the shouts of *"Vive la Nation!"* Lafayette was the man of Paris. His whole soul was directed toward a constitution that would give the people their rights and privileges. He was elected by acclamation general of the Parisian militia, and this army he transformed into the National Guard. The great Constitution was now made, and the nation rose to the defense of the Constitution. The French everywhere began to form a national guard, and the power passed from the throne into the hands of the people. The green cockade had passed away. The blue and red cockade had done its work. It was time for a new cockade. What one? The white. The color of the banners of the Maid of Orleans. Who should give the new cockade to liberty?

Lafayette!

"I bring you," said Lafayette to the new government of Paris, and we here use nearly his exact words—"I bring you a cockade. It will make the round of the world. It will begin an institution of civil and religious liberty which will

triumph over the old forms of Europe.   This institution will compel arbitrary governments to
follow it or to be overthrown.   I bring you the
white cockade."

The white cockade flew.   Paris was white.   A
German who was in Paris vividly describes the
scene: " I should not know how to express my
feelings," he said, "when, for the first time, I saw
the white cockade on the hats and caps of all I
met—citizens, peasants, children and old men,
priests and beggars, and when I could read the
pride upon the joyous foreheads, in the presence
of men of other countries, I could have wished to
clasp in my arms the first who presented themselves before me.   For as they were no longer
Frenchmen, and for the moment my companions
and I were no longer German, I am a man, I said,
and nothing which concerns humanity is foreign
to me.   So said we all."

So the white cockade became the star of two
revolutions and these revolutions were destined to
change the world.

CHAPTER X.

THE DECLARATION OF THE RIGHTS OF MAN.

REVOLUTIONS occur in summer; great deeds are born of the summer, and shortly before the fall of the Bastille on the memorable 14th of July, a date eternally to be celebrated, there appeared in the National Assembly that knight of human freedom, Marquis de Lafayette, with the sublime words, "We must make a declaration of the rights of man!" As he had gone to America as a knight, to champion liberty in the New World, and had there met Jefferson, the author of the Declaration of Independence, the words thrilled France.

The Assembly had asked the king to remove the army from Paris, since it menaced their freedom, and the king had replied that instead of removing the soldiers he would appoint another city for the meetings of the Assembly. These things we have already related.

The people were determined to secure their freedom at once and forever. The example of America rose before them, and they arose above themselves. They echoed Lafayette: "We must have a declaration of the rights of man."

The voice of Lafayette rang through France. He was awaited as the genius of liberty in the Assembly. All eyes were bent upon him as often as his tall form arose in that body of human fate. He had the spirit but not the pen of Jefferson. But the most noble sentiments began to fall from his lips after the Bastille fell, and the revolution was ripe. The declaration of the RIGHTS OF MAN came, and was formally made by the Assembly, August 26, 1789. It echoed the Declaration of Independence in America, and made France free.

Its opening was grand:

" In the presence and under the auspices of the Supreme Being, we declare,

" That all men are born to equal rights, and remain free in their equity.

" These rights are liberty, property, and the resistance of tyranny.

" The principle of sovereignty resides in the

nation, and no man can exercise authority without the people's consent.

"Law is an expression of the public will."

So read the beginning of the Declaration of the Rights of Man. In that declaration the aristocracy of France fell, and the exercise of power passed into the hands of the people.

Lafayette saw that France and the United States now stood side by side as constitutional powers. He sent the key of the Bastille to Washington, and it is still shown to visitors at Mount Vernon. His grand work in the great events of mankind was now at its height; he stood on the very pinnacle of moral influence, the knight of the liberties of two worlds, and France and America rang with the shout of "Vive Lafayette! Long live Lafayette!" It did not seem then that this man would one day be plunged into the deepest of human misery; that these glorious days would be to him the dreams of the past in a dungeon, and that the world would long seek for the hiding place, where he was hidden, in vain. But there is no high life that does not spring from or go down into the depths. The knight of liberty is soon to become the prisoner of

Olmütz, and one true heart of an American is to be the agent to deliver him from the dungeon. How did these things occur?

The mother of Francis K. Huger, the boy whom Lafayette met on his landing in America, still lived in the Carolinas, and the widow gave her life to the development and education of her son. The boy was growing up manly and noble, with the heroic traits of his father and uncles.

One day, as he had returned on a vacation, the same orderly who had brought to the family the news of Lafayette's arrival with an army at Newport, and of the surrender of Lord Cornwallis at Yorktown, again rode up to the grand old plantation house. The widow and her son came out to meet him.

" It is now as in days before," said the widow, " I hope you bring as good news."

" Yes," said the orderly ; " and it is Lafayette again."

The widow looked down toward that ever to be remembered coast where Lafayette, then not arrived at the estate of manhood, and Baron de Kalb, who gave his life for our country, had made their vow to achieve liberty for America or to perish.

"Lafayette?" said the young man; "I can imagine what it is—he has made France a republic like our own; France has become America."

"France has made her Declaration of Independence, and the author of that declaration is Lafayette. The French call this act of their National Assembly the Declaration of the Rights of Man. Lafayette has been made the commander of the National Guard of France, and the National Assembly under his leadership is now at work upon a constitution."

"He will repeat in France his work in America," said young Huger; "and make himself the hero of two worlds and the Washington of France. I wonder if I will ever see him again."

"That is not unlikely, my son," said the widow. "You will complete your education abroad, and then travel over Europe. It is not unlikely that you may then meet Lafayette."

"Meet him—if I can but see him I shall be content. He will be then the most glorious man in the world!"

"We cannot be sure, my son. The leaders of

great events sometimes meet with reverses and
have their dark days. I hope that when you see
him, should this happen, you will find him as full
of honors as of glorious deeds. Come in," she
said to the orderly.

"No, no. I am on my way. We have twice
cheered here for Lafayette. Let us cheer again
in memory of fifteen years ago. What say you,
Francis, do you remember the white cockade?"

"I have kept it."

"You may have occasion to wear it again, some
day. Lafayette has given the white cockade
to the army of France."

"All Americans will wear it again, should he
ever visit us!" said Huger.

"Which I hope he may," said the widow.

"So say we all," said the orderly. "Three
cheers for the hero of liberty!" and saying this,
he rode away.

From this pleasant scene in the Carolinas we
may go back to Paris, and behold Lafayette now
at the height of his influence and glory.

The Bastille fell on July 14, 1789. The Revolution had gone on, producing the Constitution.

On the 14th of July, 1790, occurred one of the

grandest festivals of liberty the world has ever seen ; all France, as it were, assembled to see the king take the oath of allegiance to the Constitution, and to dance at night on the ruins of the Bastille. It was to be a great day in the life of Lafayette. It was probably the happiest day he ever saw, except the one when Yorktown fell. He himself was to swear fidelity to the Constitution into which he had put his heart, in the presence of all the people.

All was in preparation for the grand fête on the 14th of July. The Commune of Paris had invited representatives from all the people of France to be present to conclude with the Parisian deputies a treaty of federation. The National Guard had filled the country and the National Assembly had decreed that this great, popular army should send one delegate for each two hundred men. An address had been issued to Frenchmen that had these stirring words :

"Ten months have flown since from the conquered walls of the Bastille arose the cry, 'We are free!' The anniversary of this event approaches ; assemble, and let the shout go up, 'We are brothers!'"

The proclamation not only aroused all France, but excited Europe.

There was a persecuted Jew in Vienna named Malan. He had brooded long over the wrongs of his race, and his soul cried out for liberty. He was a money changer and he was making a journey toward Metz when he heard the news of the address of the Commune. The words thrilled him. "We are free! We are brothers!" He resolved to visit Paris and see the fête.

Old Malan came on with the French deputation from Metz. It was a glorious company, and marched singing a song that thrilled the air:
"Ah:

> " Ça ira, ça.ira, ça ira,
> Celui qui s'élève, on l'abaissera
> Celui qui s'abissa on l'élevera ! "

The song is not easily translated—the " Ça ira " literally means "It will come," or " It is well," but in this connection had the force of " Let it go on !"

> " The humble shall be exalted,
> The exalted shall be abased ! "

Our own Franklin is said to have furnished the refrain for this song. He had said in Paris that

"Ça ira, ça ira!"

tyrants, if they resisted the people, would one day hang from the lamp posts. "It will come—*Ça ira!*"

The old Jew's heart glowed with the sentiment of liberty and equality. He sang as lustily as the Frenchmen.

> "Ça ira, ça ira, ça ira,
> The humble shall be exalted,
> The exalted shall be abased!"

As he approached Paris what a scene met his eyes! The world seemed on the move. Everywhere, like the white rose of France, was seen the white cockade.

The Champs de Mars was a plain near Paris. The Commune had erected there a high altar of liberty, and the people of Paris resolved to widen the plain for the celebration of the Bastille's fall.

Many went to work to do this, the rich and the poor together, singing as they marched and labored,

> "Ça ira, ça ira, ça ira!"

The work was begun by fifteen thousand men. On the 7th of July it had not been accomplished.

The plain must be made a valley and the July sun was burning fast, and the 14th was near.

Three hundred thousand men and women rushed to the plain to complete the work. The rich and the titled sang, "Ça ira"; the poor sang with them,

"Let it go on, let it go on,
  The humble shall be exalted,
  The exalted shall be abased !"

The plain became a valley and the great altar of liberty rose in the sun. On that altar the king, compelled by the people, was expected to take the oath.

The enthusiasm grew. The workmen of Paris who labored days came to the plain to continue their toil by night. The warm nights glowed, and under the moon and stars rang but one voice,

"Let it go on ! let it go on ! "

The day came. The sky was a blaze of splendor. The Champs de Mars was ready. France had assembled, and the white rose bloomed on the heads of the representatives of an army of three millions of men.

The king trembled. He no longer ruled the

people, but the people ruled him. The assembly filled the plain.

There was an immense procession; old men and children joined it as in the days of Greece. Music pealed, flowers were strewn. The great Talleyrand, surrounded by two hundred ecclesiastics, in tri-colored girdles, led the religious rites.

All was glory, expectation, and joy.

Up the high altar walked the tall form of Lafayette, sword in hand. The sword gleamed in the sun, and then was laid on the altar. The hearts of the people were thrilled and the air was rent.

Then came the poor trembling king to the people, not to the altar, but to the estrade, and said:

"I, King of the French, swear to uphold the Constitution decreed by the National Assembly and accepted by me."

At night France danced on the ruin of the Bastille, and cried, "We are brothers!"

Fête followed fête for days and nights. The people were delirious with joy. They marched everywhere singing,

> "It is well, it is well!
> Ça ira, ça ira, ça ira."

The Constitution was made ; the king had sworn to protect it ; the people were free and brothers.

" The world is upset," said the Jew, " but can these things last ? Will the new liberty ever reach me and my people ? "

He did not know.

He saw Lafayette go up the steps of the altar of liberty ; he saw the sword of the great apostle of liberty gleam, and drop upon the altar, and he went back to Vienna singing,

> " Ça ira, ça ira, ça ira,
> The humble shall be exalted,
> The exalted shall be abased."

CHAPTER XI.

THE BLACK COCKADE.

OULD anyone have dreamed previous to 1792 that Lafayette, the hero of two worlds, would become an exile, a prisoner, and suffer long in dungeons? That he would need the sympathy of all the people in the world, to whom his struggle for human freedom had endeared him? We repeat the question. Strange as it may seem, there came to Paris and France the day of the *black* cockade.

Lafayette was the maker and defender of constitutional liberty. He had sworn to support the constitution of France.

But the Jacobin clubs became the leading party in Paris. They were opposed to every order of the nobility, and Lafayette gave up his title of marquis and was glad to be known as a plain citizen. But these clubs, which largely formed the Commune, found the constitution a barrier to their wild schemes of the rule of the people. In the so-called revolution of August 10, 1792, the constitutional throne was overthrown ; the royal family were made prisoners, and there was begun the awful period of blood in which one faction succeeded another in slaughter, called the Reign of Terror. The guillotine which ended the lives of the king and queen did its work until France was sick of blood.

Lafayette had opposed the rise of the Commune. As soon as this body had overturned the throne and had broken the constitution, the revolutionists demanded his arrest. He had gone to the army that was guarding the frontier. To allow himself to be arrested would end his career. He resolved to leave the country, to go to Holland, and thence sail again for America. On the 19th of August, he and some French officers came to Rochefort, which was neutral ground, and where they expected to be protected by the law of nations. They here met a detachment of Austrian hussars, of the army threatening the frontier. Lafayette sent word to the commanding officer, that he and his friends had been proscribed by France, and were seeking an asylum in a neutral territory, and were about to embark for America.

"And who is your leader?" demanded the Austrian officer.

"General Lafayette."

"Then he is my prisoner."

"But we are on neutral ground."

"That matters not. The King of Prussia and the Emperor of Austria look upon Lafayette as a common enemy of royalty; the Queen of France herself holds him to be an enemy; and he shall never pass out of my lines until I have instructions from my superiors. No, no—we have indeed captured a rare bird, and he will be caged."

"But the law of nations?"

"There is no law of nations for such a prisoner as Lafayette. That man has shaken the earth, and now he, too, may tremble."

Lafayette was at once arrested, and placed under guard. The King of Prussia, violating the law of nations, commanded his imprisonment. Despotism had now the great leader of human freedom in its power.

But his arrest, in violation of the law of nations, was a shock to the world. Petitions for the release of Lafayette began to pour in to the Prussian court.

What was to be done with the constitution maker ?

He must be sent out of the Prussian dominions, and he must somewhere be secretly imprisoned, where the world could not know where he was, and where his friends could not find him.   Where was there such a place ?   Where was there a dungeon that none could find, and whose doors were silence ?

Where ?

CHAPTER XII.

FRANCIS K. HUGER grew up a manly boy with the culture and refinements of the youth of early Southern life. The Huger families of South Carolina had sent their sons abroad to be educated, and although his father was dead, his mother desired him to receive the most liberal education in Europe. So he sailed away from his Southern home, consecrated to fame by the vow of Lafayette, and the years of the closing century found him a traveling student in England and on the Continent.

As he was one day traveling in provincial France, on his way to Germany, a strange sight met his eye, and a glorious outburst of music fell upon his ears. A detachment of French volunteers came marching through the town. The streets filled with excited people, and these people were led by a woman in white, who at times tossed her hands wildly into the air and cried, "*Liberté!*"

The band ceased playing, and the drums led the march. The detachment halted in the public square, before the Hôtel de Ville. It was a calm, sunny day; a fountain was playing, and the square and the balconies were filled with a crowd that seemed to grow and grow.

The soldiers rested. The woman in white, who had been leading the people, came and stood upon the high steps of the fountain, and lifting her dark but heroic face to the sun, and waving her hand aloft, cried, "*Liberté!*"

A great shout followed.

"Now!" she cried, waving her hand again. "Now, ye sons of France, awake! The day of glory has arrived!"

The band started up the same grand song that had thrilled the young traveler when he first heard the air:

"Ye sons of Freedom, wake to glory."

The chorus set the whole town to singing. The balconies sang and shouted, the chorus was repeated over and over again.

"The day of glory has arrived."

The detachment contained
a company of soldiers from
Marseilles. It was the wonderful Marseilles Hymn of
liberty, that the people
had been singing. It
had been composed by a
young musical soldier,
in an hour of inspiration,
it is said, as he was
falling asleep and roused
up again, and the mus-
ic indicates this mood.
However this legend may
be, the song was filling
and thrilling France. It
was the war cry of liberty.

But liberty now was
passing the bounds of
law, and was becoming
the enemy to liberty.
True liberty is the right
to do right, not the right
to follow personal feel-
ing. The young traveler

listened, and he thought
of Lafayette.

He stepped up to an
officer who was bedecked
with stars, tricolors, and
cockade, and said:

"Pardon! I am a traveler.
Where is Lafayette?"

"General Lafayette?"

"The Marquis de La-
fayette".

"Pardon me. We have
done with marqueses
here. Lafayette is no longer
a general. The Jacobins
have voted him an
enemy; his soldiers have
turned Jacobins, and he
has gone over the border.
He is lost; has disap-
peared, he has been cap-
tured, or perhaps, he
has gone to ___

America.   He was a friend of America during the war.   Are you from America?"

"Yes."

"Did you know Lafayette?"

"I once met him when a boy."

"He led the National Guard in the days of the constitution.   He defended the constitution, but those days are passed.   The people rule; the day of glory has arrived!"

The soldiers were summoned to form into line. The glittering detachment began to move.   The woman in white again took her place at the head of the people.   The band struck up again the same thrilling air:

"Ye sons of Freedom, wake to glory!"

And so the soldiers, followed by a great crowd and led by a band with the woman in white, passed out of the town.

Had France gone mad?

Where was Lafayette?

CHAPTER XIII.

THE PATRIOTIC PARROT.

NOW old Malan can live again." So said an old Jew, in a little narrow lane near one of the grand streets in Vienna. He had gone to live there in the early part of the century, this very queer Hungarian Jew, named Malan, whom we saw at the féte of the Bastille. He was one of the strangest people in Vienna. There is usually something wrong about what is strange, but there was nothing wrong about Malan. He was a money changer, but he was scrupulously honest. He was learned, and he had heard that there was a man named George Washington who had contended for the equal rights of all men in the far Western world. He had hoped that some such man might rise for the liberation of his own scattered race.

There was a small garden at the back of his house, and in it was a lime tree, and there old Malan used to sit and talk on summer days. He

had a parrot which he had bought at a Mediter-
ranean port, because it had been brought by a
ship from the Western world. The bird had a
blue breast and green wings with red feathers, and
he loved it because he had heard that another
patriot from the land from which the bird came,
by the name of Bolivar, was also contending for
the same equality that Washington had secured
for the United States of the West.

Old Malan had lost his wife, and his children
had married and gone to live in other countries.
He had been rich, but he had lost his property by
a persecution of the Jews in Hungary, and he used
to speak of himself as one who had been dead.
When he first lost his property he was very sad.
A country that could deprive him of his rights
because of his race was no better to him than a
tomb. The children used to gather about him
under the lime tree.

"Why do you come to see old Malan?" he
would say, "Do you not know that he is dead?"

"Yes, but you are talking," said one.

"I am talking as one dead. There will never
be any life for poor old Malan until the Jews
have equal rights with mankind. I hear they

have gained such things in the Western world, now. If I could go to the West, I would go to heaven."

" No, old Malan," once said a little girl, "you would be in another world, but not in heaven."

He looked up to the blue patch of sky.

"I was once rich, children, now look at my hands."

Here he opened his hands.

"I once thought that I had friends, but no one knows who his friends are until he has nothing. I once had friends, but where are they now? Where?"

The children would gather close to him as he would talk in this way, for he was benevolent in spirit and they loved him.

Then he would begin to tell them of what he had heard of the wonderful country in the West, where all the people were free to do right.

"Children, the old prophets saw that land," he would say. " If I were only there, I would own the earth, the sky, and the stars. The person whose rights are protected has everything. But what is the use for me to gain means? The world is against me and it will take it all away."

He dreamed of the Western world. One day

he had traveled down to a port town by the sea, where he met an American ship and bought the parrot, which he was told had came from Trinidad. The parrot spoke many words, as these parrots do, and was very affectionate, as the blue front, green parrots of South America are.

Two delightful things that the parrot said were:

"Hurrah for Washington!"

"Hurrah for Bolivar!"

The old Jew took the bird to his garden, and the children multiplied under the lime tree on summer evenings to hear it talk.

"Hurrah for Washington!" the bird would scream.

"What Washington?" the old Jew would ask.

"George," would answer the bird.

"Hush, that is treason!" the old Jew would answer.

The Jew and the parrot were the warmest friends. The attachment between the lonely old man and the excitable bird became so great as to be a matter of public curiosity.

One day a young American traveler came to see the bird. The man was delighted to be saluted with:

"Hurrah for Washington!"

He answered "Hurrah for Lafayette!"

The bird did not answer, but rushed nervously about the cage.

"Polly wants to come out!" said the bird.

"Hurrah for Lafayette!" said the traveler.

The bird rushed around the cage, and at last said:

"Hurrah for Bolivar!"

"Here, stranger, sit down," said Malan, "where do you come from?"

"From America—I am a traveler. It is a pleasant thing to hear your parrot cheer for our country's hero. Where did it learn these words?"

"On an American ship, sailing about the world. Your Washington was a great man, I hear; a Pericles, Cincinnatus, Maccabeus. Is it true that all men in your country are free?"

"Free to do everything that does not harm society."

"Just as though there were no law?"

"There is no law in a free country for those who do right, my good friend."

"No, and there never ought to be. Do you mean to tell me that Jews in your country have their rights like other people?"

"Certainly, my friend ; just the same as other people."

"And is their property safe?"

"Just as safe as other people's, I am pleased to say."

"How did you get your rights?"

"We made a Declaration of Rights. Lafayette made a like declaration in France."

The man looked up to the bird and said, "Hurrah for Lafayette!

"How old Malan would love to go to your country! But I don't suppose that I ever shall. How did that Declaration begin?"

The stranger placed his hands behind him, and paced to and fro under the lime tree.

"Like this."

"Children, you be still, listen."

"Hurrah for Washington!" said the South American bird.

"The Declaration began like this," said the traveler, in a voice like a solemn chant: "'When, in the course of human events,——'"

"'When, in the course of human events,'" repeated the Jew in a Hungarian accent.

"'It becomes necessary for one people to dissolve the political bands which have connected them with another, and to assume, among the powers of the earth, the separate and equal station to which the laws of nature and of nature's God entitle them, a decent respect to the opinions of mankind requires that they should declare the causes which impel them to the separation.'"

The traveler turned around and looked old Malan in the face. The blue-fronted parrot peered from its cage, and the children stood with open mouths.

"'We hold,'" quoted the traveler, "'these truths to be self-evident.'"

"What?" asked old Malan.

"'We hold these truths to be self-evident, that all men are created equal.'"

"Do I hear my ears?" said the Jew, "that all men are created equal; the old prophets said that. Our God told that to Jonah more than two thousand years ago. 'All men are created equal.' Why cannot I go to the West? But look at my hands, my hair, my beard. They are thin, very thin. But go on."

"'That all men are created equal, and are

endowed by their Creator with certain inalienable rights.'"

"'Certain inalienable rights,'" repeated the Jew.

"'Among these are life, liberty, and the pursuit of happiness.'"

"Stranger !——"

The Jew rose trembling. His eyes were streaming with tears.

"Stranger—there is a land like that in the West? I am glad that I am alive. Now old Malan can live again. And what did you say was that general's name that is fighting for the same ideas in France?"

"Lafayette. He is in exile now."

"Lafayette! I will remember him. Lafayette!"

CHAPTER XIV.

THE MYSTERIOUS TRAVELER.

AT one of the old inns in Vienna, there met, about a century ago, two students, and each was a mystery to the other. Each spoke English; one was a German and the other an American. The American was Frances K. Huger, the boy whom Lafayette met when he landed in America.

People having like sympathies are attracted toward each other, even before they know each others hearts. We are not sure that they are not so attracted even before they meet; life has sympathetic atmospheres through which influences pass like telegrams, it may be; and these two students were one in heart, though one had a purpose he was slow to confess. They were both versed in the political condition of America and France, and their conversation turned on politics as often as they met.

One serene day they rode together out of the

city on to the plain toward Wiener Wald. The sky was a clear splendor; the plain was bright with flowers, and the mountains stood in somber shadow, cool and green. They stopped to rest at last under some wayside trees, where they discussed the recent dark events in France and the so-called Revolution of August 10th, by which the constitution was overthrown.

The German student's name was Bollman—Eric Bollman. He was a physician and had studied under famous teachers. He was an ardent republican, and he said to his new American friend that day, after an earnest conversation :

" I have a secret that I would share with you, if I dared."

"You certainly can trust me, my friend. I have never sought anyone's confidence, nor been untrue to my own honor or my family name."

"I have carried this secret alone as long as I can bear it ; I have for a long time been seeking someone to share it with me. My heart tells me that you are the man. People may deceive us, but our own instincts do not lie to us ; we have an inner life that is true to us."

" May I ask, whom does the secret concern, my friend ? "

" To speak that name would reveal to you much. There is a new mystery in the world, as deep as that of the Man in the Iron Mask or the hiding of King Richard the Lion-hearted in a prison on the Danube."

His horse became restive, and the young student circled round the trees, to bring the animal to a quiet.

" Richard was confined in an Austrian prison, was he not ? " said the young American, " and Blondel found him by his harp, so the story runs. It is as good as a story."

" There is a prisoner hidden in Austria to-day, more noble than was ever Richard the Lion-hearted, and a man whose genius is creating a new world for mankind."

" Where is he ? " asked the American student.

" I do not know ; the world does not know."

" Then you should be a Blondel and find him," said the American.

" Yes, so it would seem ; but I am not sure that it is not you who should do this duty to a hero of heroes. and to mankind."

" I ? "

"Yes, you, my good friend."

"I am simply an American traveler, and no Blondel. I came to Europe to finish my education, to see the world, and to return to my own country, which, thank God, is free. We have no castle prisons for such men there, and all that I see here convinces me of the wisdom of the government of my own United States of America, where every man is free to pursue anything that is useful to himself or the world. There is no law there for anyone who follows the law of his moral being. I am glad, more—I rejoice in my heart—that my country *is* free."

"To whom, my friend, do you owe your liberties?"

"To the people."

"Who were your leaders into this new state of equality?"

"Washington and Lafayette."

"Lafayette—he has been a hero in both worlds; he made the decisive stroke for the freedom of America, and has as nobly defended the constitutional liberties of France. Did you ever meet Lafayette?"

"Yes, my friend, but it was in America, many years ago, when I was a boy, scarcely more than three years of age. I used to hear about him dur-ing the war, and it thrilled my heart when I learned that he had landed a second time in our country, that time bringing with him an army. Washington ordered the officers of the American army to wear the white cockade in honor of that event. I remember, too, the time when a courier came flying toward our plantation house, say-ing, 'Cornwallis is taken!' How my heart beat when I first heard the news of the surrender of Yorktown!"

"Yorktown? my dear young friend. Who won the siege at Yorktown?"

"Lafayette, under the direction of Wash-ington."

"It was he, was it, who made your heart thrill when a boy?"

"Yes, I have ever followed his career with admiration. Every man has his hero; he was the hero of my boyhood; after Washington. He is so now."

"He is mine!"

"He once dandled me on his knee, and I asked

him questions that awakened his interest. I was a talkative child."

"That was many years ago?"

"Yes, many; my father was alive then. He fell in the war."

"Is it possible that you knew Lafayette in that way? How strange it is that we should meet here."

Dr. Bollman turned his horse and looked back on Vienna, gleaming in the sun. He rode around the trees again and said——

"Your name is Huger?"

"Yes, Francis Kinlock Huger."

"You are from the Carolinas in America?"

"I am proud to say that I am."

"Your family were patriots in the Revolution?"

"All of them were."

"And you knew Lafayette when a boy?"

"I did. I only vaguely remember him and our curious interview, when I was sitting on his knee."

"You honor his course in life?"

"I do; and I love the man with a patriotic love; not with any romantic or sentimental affec-

tion, although we Carolinians are regardful of
romance and sentiment, but with the love that
those who sympathize in the same cause feel for
each other. It is the great love ; it is higher than
all loves. I loved him when I first met him as a
boy and that attraction has never ceased. His
exploits in America used to thrill me, as an
orderly or courier brought the news."

"What would you do for that same hero of
your heart, if he were in peril?"

"You may believe it, or not, but what I say is
true. I would give all that I have or am to serve
such a man, whose own service had been that of
my country and humanity."

The mountains gleamed afar, and the shadows
on the plain grew purple and long. The châ-
teaus with their orchards changed the picture
that lay behind them in the sinking sun as
the shadows grew dark, and the young American said :

"We must ride back. But you have awakened
my curiosity, and you should now satisfy it, if you
trust my honor. You may safely confide in me ;
there was never a Huger who was untrue to any
man. You, indeed, are a mysterious traveler, but

I believe you to have an honest purpose. Who is the hidden prisoner in Austria of whom you have been speaking?"

"My friend, this hour surpasses the mysteries of fiction; how did I ever meet you here? That prisoner, that hidden prisoner, sir, is General Lafayette!"

Huger reined his horse.

"Then we must rescue him. How did you know that he was a prisoner in this country!"

"I will tell you. There is some strange fate that is leading us both."

"There seems to be."

Young Huger shed tears.

"America comes back to me," he said, "my old Carolinian home; my father, who was killed in the Revolution; and that summer night when there came to our house that strange French general. Dr. Bollman, listen! *That* very night Lafayette and Baron de Kalb swore under the moon and stars on the shores near our house that they would give their lives and fortunes to the cause of American liberty, Dr. Bollman, we are two students about the age Lafayette was at that time. Let us here make a vow to liberate Lafayette. I pledge my honor before Heaven to do this thing."

The German student lifted his face to the sky. "I pledge my honor before God to do this thing," he said firmly.

The two students clasped each other's hands and rode back to Vienna in the sunset.

CHAPTER XV.

THEY had a common secret and purpose and they went to the same hotel.

That night they secured the same apartments. They went from their supper to their rooms. They sat down together, but they did not soon light the lamps. The military bands were playing in the distance and the streets were deserted and silent. The twinkle of the lamps and the watchmen's lanterns only relieved the quiet of the darkness.

"We are alone," said young Huger, "and now I wish you to tell me how you came to find out where Lafayette was imprisoned. I thought that he was merely detained in Prussia."

"I will tell you all of a strange story. Some unknown power, as I said, has seemed to lead me. Did you ever meet Lally-Tollendal?"

"No."

"He is a friend of mine. I came to know him

in Paris. His hero, too, is Lafayette. One day,
amid the butcheries of the Commune, he came to
me and told me that Lafayette had been secretly
imprisoned and that it was his conviction that as
I was a traveler I should make it my mission to
find *where* he was imprisoned. That I have
done."

"How? How, my dear friend?"

"I am a poor student. I went to Hamburg.
I found that Lafayette had been imprisoned first
at Luxembourg, and he had been taken in a
common cart to Wessel on the Rhine. Here he
had been placed in a cold, damp cell, and had
fallen sick from neglect and exposure. His hair
had come off, and his flesh had wasted. He had
been a great sufferer. Then came to the King of
Prussia the petitions from England and America
for his release. They annoyed the king. He
resolved to send him to a secret prison in Austria,
for it is the oft-repeated statement among the
leading courts of the Continent that the 'liberty
of Lafayette is incompatible with the peace of
royal governments.'

"So I learned that he had been sent to a secret
prison in Austria. I had not the money to go to

Austria ; but I was resolved to find the place of his imprisonment and I have done so."

" How did you raise the money ? "

"A student has one thing—books.   I sold mine, but they did not bring me in enough for my journey.   So I intrusted my plan to a rich mer-chant ; he favored me and lent me the means of going to Austria, as a student traveler."

" I have means ; my folks are rich planters, and I will share my purse with you as far as I can. I am nothing to myself now—nothing to myself— in this cause."

"Thank you ; I have less need of money now than of the courage of a friend.   I am, as you know, a medical student, and I have my papers to that effect with me.   I can easily make the acquaintance of the surgeons of the fortresses where military and state prisoners are kept.   I believe that Lafayette is confined in the state prison of the Fortress of Olmütz."

"Do you know any of the surgeons of that fortress ? "

"Yes, I have been there and met one of them.   I have letters of introduction which I may use to make the acquaintance of medical men at Olmütz, and so, of the surgeons of that fortress."

" I would use them at once."

" That I have already done. I will tell you how I did it. I had this curious plan. I went to the surgeon of the fortress, and asked him if he would take a pamphlet from me to the state prisoner, Lafayette."

" But you were not sure that Lafayette was there ?"

" No, but I knew that if he were not, the surgeon would at once show surprise at my request and say no such man was there. If he said nothing my opinion would be confirmed."

" I hope that you were successful. Your story thrills me."

" I was. I said to myself, it will be a great point gained to find out *where* Lafayette is. France does not know, his own family do not know. England and America would again seek his release if they knew. Those countries do not know at what court to make their appeal. It is the plan of these courts that it shall be so. I am going to Olmütz to-day. Will you go with me ?"

"If you find where Lafayette is, we must rescue him."

"We will at least make his rescue by England and America possible."

"No nobler patriot ever lived; others have fought for their own country, but he fought for humanity. Yes, I will go; I could not stay!"

"True. When the king of Prussia saw that he was holding his prisoner against the moral opinion of the world he attempted to bribe him. He sent a messenger to say, 'If you will unite with us against *your* enemies in France, you shall be released.'"

"And what did Lafayette answer? I need not ask."

"He was in extreme suffering at the time. He was worn with sickness, and lack of food and fire."

"Yes, but what did he say?"

"He said, 'Never will I take up arms against my countrymen! My name is Lafayette!' These last words were his own, as I have received the information. 'My name is Lafayette!'"

"And my name is Francis Kinlock Huger."

"And mine, Eric Bollman."

" And mine stands for honor, I hope."

" And mine."

"So, all I have, my life and fortune, all, all in the name of America, my own free and happy America, I offer for the rescue of Lafayette ! This is the mystery of my life. How will it end?"

"*Hurrah for Washington !*"

" What was that ?"

" It came from the garden in the lane."

" It sounded like a parrot."

" The Jew has a parrot."

" What Jew ?"

" The money changer."

"I imagined that I heard someone in that garden say *Lafayette.*"

"So did I."

" It could not be."

CHAPTER XVI.

THE SILENT SURGEON.

TELL me," said young Huger, "this story more fully. How came you to *know* that Lafayette was imprisoned at Olmütz? You said you knew. How is Olmütz situated?"

"It is a strange story. I have told only a part of it. But first let me tell you where Olmütz is. It is in the province of Moravia, about a hundred miles from here. It is a powerful fortress and as gloomy as it is powerful.

"The waters of the Moravia hem it in. The walls are of stone, some twelve feet thick. The windows are so deep that the sun's rays can seldom enter them. The cells of the fortress prison are not only dark, but damp and cold. The town is pleasant, but the fortress is terrible.

"This fortress is a relic of the barbarism of the Middle Ages. Of all the places in Europe it is the one where a hidden prisoner of state would be the least likely to be found.

"I went to Olmütz, as I told you, on the suspicion that Lafayette might be hidden there.   I
presented myself to the hospital surgeon of the
fortress.

"'I am a German traveler, sir,' I said, 'and I
wish to see the military hospitals of Europe, and
to study their methods and the experiments that
are made on the patients.'

"'You are welcome, sir,' he said.   'I like a
young student who is alive to these things.   A
medical man cannot have too much knowledge,
and the hospital is the true school of medical
science.'

"'There is one subject in which I am especially
interested,' I continued.   'It is the effect which
imprisonment has upon refined and delicate consti-
tutions, as of prisoners of state.   How it affects
their hearts, brains, muscles, and blood, their
digestion and sleep.   The inferences from such a
study are most important.   The influence is different from that of the sick chamber; or even
from that of the confinement of the insane.'

"'I see you have a very interesting subject in
hand,' said the surgeon.

"'Very.   Since tens of thousands of people in

every country are engaged in occupations that confine them to one room. Such a life develops peculiar diseases. Melancholia is one of them ; a subtile kind of poisoning of the blood from an excess of acids may be another.'

"'Such a life is as great a peril to the mind as to the body,' said the surgeon. 'Let me tell you some of my observations of the effects of a sedentary life on prisoners of state. This is a secret prison where many of the prisoners are shut out from all knowledge of the world. The world is dead to them.'

"'Tell me about some particular prisoners, and the effects of this tomb-like solitude on their bodies and minds,' said I. We two talked long on this most interesting topic. It was night and the hour grew late.

"'I must go now,' I said. 'I have seldom been so much interested in anything as in the narra- tives of your experience. By the way, you have a French prisoner of state, who used to know some of my old friends—General Lafayette.'

"The surgeon stared, attempted to speak, but made no answer.

"'His imprisonment must have affected his

health and spirits, and I have a pamphlet here that contains accounts of his old friends. I am sure that it would greatly interest him. Will you hand it to him?'

"The surgeon stood like a statue. There was a puzzled look in his eyes and face that seemed to say, 'How do you know these things? Who has told you of them?'

"He at length began to pace to and fro impatiently. He stopped at times as if to ask a question. But he had well learned the instructions commanding silence. So he uttered not a word. But that silence had its tongue. No voice could be plainer.

"'You may like to read the pamphlet,' said I, 'and afterward hand it to the general. If you do so, you need not mention my name. He does not know me. I would like to talk with you at some future time on the effect that confinement has had on his mind and temperament. He has been used to a very active life and much excitement. Good-night.'

"The surgeon bowed in a stately way, but did not speak a word. And yet he had spoken again, and the last silence bore witness to the first."

" Lafayette is his prisoner," said Dr. Bollman. As he passed out into the still air of the night, Huger followed him, but this repeated story did not satisfy him. Had his new friend proof of these things ?

As he passed down the street the moon hung over the towers. The sentinels were passing to and fro, and a great dark clock announced the late hour.

They felt the loneliness of the situation.

" The end of a high purpose is victory," said Huger.

As they passed along they thought again they heard the name of Lafayette spoken in a back garden.

" It cannot be," said the doctor.

" *Three cheers for Washington !* "

" What was that ? "

" The Jew's parrot."

" We must call on the Jew," said the doctor.

" He is an acquaintance of mine," said Huger.

CHAPTER XVII.

THE BAG OF GOLD.

WHILE Huger was living in Vienna he used often to meet that curious character, Malan, the Jew. The latter could speak French well and a little English, and he was commonly known at home as old Money Bags, or Malan, the money changer.

Old and thin, he had the usual long hair and beard of his race. But his face was so benevolent and winning that the young American was attracted to him, and when he wished for directions in plans of travel he used to consult him, and so came to know him well.

To Malan, the Jew, the wisdom of life lay in proverbs, and he enforced his ordinary talk, even in business, with proverbs of his own and many lands.

"I hope I do not trouble you," said young Huger one day, as he went up to the Jew's exchange, which projected from the old house under some cool trees.

"How trouble me, my wanderer?"

"By asking you so many questions."

"It makes me not poorer by trying to answer them. But he that would seek many things will find trouble. You will have trouble some day. What we do not see, do not know, does not harm us. Herein is wisdom."

"I have come to ask you if there is any danger of my saying openly here that I am an American? Would it be better for me to seek English protection?"

"No, no; it is best always for a man to go about for just what he is. If he do not, the world is sure to find him out. What is the sun for? What are one's eyes for?"

"But I am told that General Lafayette, who fought for our country, has been hidden in some prison in these countries, without process of law, because his principles were incompatible with royal governments."

"That may be, but you are not a Lafayette. The goose does not soar to the sky like an eagle and get shot."

"No, I am not a Lafayette or an eagle. But I may be suspected of holding the principles of Lafayette and of being an eagle."

"No, no!" said the Jew; "the world does not mix the birds up in that way. But do you want I should tell you what you are thinking about? Old Malan can tell most people what they are thinking about. Herein is wisdom. Most of the people who come here think that I am a Jew, and will cheat them. But they are mistaken. He that cheats another, cheats himself. I am an honest man. So you see they are mistaken.

"Now would you like to have me tell you what you are thinking about? I can. You are thinking that I am talking in this way to take some advantage of you, but I am not. Old Malan would treat you just as though you were old Malan. The way to travel in this world is to turn to the right and go straight ahead, and you will get there!"

"Where?"

"That is what I would like to know myself. It is hard to tell where we came from or where we are going to, but of this you and I can be sure, that it is well with the honest man; he is on the right road, and he will always find it better farther on."

Old Malan lifted his thin hands to his head. The sun sifted through the lime trees and he looked into the open face of the young American.

"Young man, I am reading you. You come from a country that has made the people free. The old prophets saw such a country. Never hesitate wherever you may be to say that you are an American. Why? Do you ask old Malan why? An American is a brother to all men, and all men one day will be free."

"I am proud of my country."

"Proud, and well you may be. Young man, I love you; old Malan, the Jew, loves you, but perhaps you do not care for the love of Malan, the Jew. I love you because you come from the land where all are free! Think what my people have suffered. You may not like my race, but we spring from God, and a Jew is never ashamed to say that he is a Jew. We never forget our origin, and we are true hearted to our own. The best thing in the world is to be true hearted. Herein is wisdom."

Huger turned away convinced of the old man's

sincerity. The Jew followed him with his eye, his face beaming with a kind of brotherly feeling. Presently he called after him :

"Young traveler from the West; you, young traveler——"

The student stopped.

" If ever you are in trouble, come to me. Old Malan will treat you like his own heart. Old Malan wants money, but he does not want yours ; he would give you money, but not take, for in giving is love. Herein is wisdom. Do not forget me. My heart has never been false to any man, and my heart is yours !"

Huger went up the street slowly, among the bright, happy people. His mind was full of Lafayette. Would it do to take old Malan, the Jew, into the secret ? He would need money to give Lafayette, and perhaps more than he could command. He went back to his hotel and met Dr. Bollman on the steps.

" Dr. Bollman, I wish to speak with you in my room. I have found a man in Vienna that I think we can intrust with our plans."

The two went to their apartments, when Dr. Bollman said : " We have need of further help.

We need a confidant in Vienna. Who is that man ? "

" He is a Jew."

" Never trust a Jew."

" Dr. Bollman, I cannot agree with you. The Jewish heart is true to its own race and to its friends. This man's heart is true to all people. The principles of universal love, justice, and liberty came from the Jewish race. Dr. Bollman, I do not think as you do."

" What is this Jew ? "

" A money changer."

" Never trust a money changer."

" And why ? It is as honorable an occupation as that of a banker. Dr. Bollman, will you go with me to-night and call on this Jew ? We will have to know how to secure money for this enterprise. It will pay you to pass the evening with him, if it be only to gather up his proverbs."

" The Jews are great on quoting proverbs," said Dr. Bollman, " but not over careful in following them. Yes, I will go. We must, as you say, have further help, and Jews, if they are grasping, are not treacherous."

That evening the two students went to Malan's

door.   He lived in a tall house, with a lonely and lofty look ; antique, with shut window blinds and unused balconies.   A single light illumined a shutter in an upper room.

They knocked and were admitted by a servant, and conducted to Malan's room.

"I have accepted your invitation," said the American traveler, "and I have brought with me a friend.   He is also a student and a traveler."

"You are welcome," said the Jew.   "Young people seek old people when they have need of them, and when they are seeking direction. Solomon said, 'O Lord, thou hast given me the choice of three things—riches, fame, and wisdom ; give me wisdom, and by it I will get the other two.'   What brings you here to-night to me ?"

"We are alone," said Dr. Bollman, "and my friend has told me that you would be a wise friend to know."

"Then it is wisdom."

"Yes, we are in need of it."

The doctor hesitated and asked : "Who is the wisest man in the world ?"

"He that overcomes the evils of his own nature

for the welfare of others. Such a man possesses his own self and the world."

"But that is not the question that brought us here."

"No, that is not the matter that brought you here. Do you want that I should tell you of what you are thinking? You are dwelling in your mind on some mystery in your life."

"Why do you say this? Have you hidden knowledge?"

"Yes, but it is the hidden eye that anyone may have. You do not come to me when the exchange is open; nor by day, but in the night, and a young student like you does not seek for an interview with an old man like me without a reason, and whatever an American may feel, a German has a race prejudice against a Jew."

"Why should he? Did not your race produce a Judas Maccabæus?"

"True, true," said the Jew, starting. "It is now all clear to me. What is the sun for? Shall I tell you of what you are thinking? Would you like to have me tell you now?"

The question startled Bollman. He looked around the room. Old faded pictures were there;

statues stood in the shadows. Here and there were carved chairs.

"Yes," said Dr. Bollman, "tell me of what I am thinking."

"I will first tell you of what you are not think-ing. You are not thinking of Judas Maccabæus, *our* hero. No, no. You are *not* thinking of *him.*"

A spinet stood at the side of the room where the Jew was sitting. He reached out his long arms, waving the sleeves of his dressing gown, and began to play, with one hand, Händel's "See, the Conquering Hero Comes." He looked into the faces of the two students almost absently, and said : "They are all gone—wife, children, and all. I am all alone, alone. Something new is com-ing to me. I can feel it coming. Come, come! Events come, the same as people. Events come, the same as strangers. Events come, but they come with a purpose. Events have souls."

He drummed the Händel air from "Judas Maccabæus" again, then leaned forward, and peered into the face of Dr. Bollman : "Now shall I tell you of what you are thinking ?"

"Yes, yes."

"You are not thinking of *my* hero, you are thinking of *your* hero. Is not that true?"

"Yes," said Dr. Bollman.

"And now, my young friend from the free people of the West, where the sun goes down, you noble heart from the new land of God, shall I tell you of whom *you* are thinking?"

"Yes, tell me. This is very strange."

"And will you answer my questions if I answer you rightly?"

"Yes; I can trust you. The spirit in my heart says so, and that spirit never lies."

"My young wanderer from the West, you are thinking of *your* hero; and shall I tell you who your hero is?"

"Yes, yes," said the young man, starting.

"Well, then; be still ye walls if ye have ears! Your hero is Lafayette. Is it not so? You promised to answer me."

"Yes; it is," said the young traveler. "Yes, it is. You *already* seem to know all."

"And you come to me for help in regard to his liberation?"

"How did you know that man and our purpose?"

"I am no romancer, I am an honest man. You spoke that name when you called before, and that word 'already' reveals much."

"My friend," said Bollman, "we have given you so much of our secret that we want your promise of secrecy, if we will make known to you all that is in our hearts."

"I would know it all soon, whether you told me directly or not. It is the slips of speech that is true language with those who have something to conceal."

"My friend, we have nothing now to conceal from you. I am seeking Lafayette, who is hidden in an Austrian prison. That prison is at Olmütz. I have come from there. I wish to release him; to set him free!"

"You are not a Frenchman?"

"No."

"You are not seeking money nor fame in this purpose?"

"No; I have thought of neither."

"What prompts you?"

"Something within."

"Yes; the spirit of events. It dwells there."

"I want your help."

"Of course. You shall have it! Here it is. I——"

The Jew arose and trimmed the lamp. He opened a carved chest and took out of it a small but heavy bag. He put the bag on the table beside the lamp. He opened the bag, untying the string. He took out a gold piece. He laid down a heavy gold coin.

"There," said he, "he who gives to what benefits all men, enriches his own soul, and that soul is the richest of all that gives away everything. He who denies himself the most, receives the most from God. We shall all be dust soon, and it is only the gold of the soul that will pass in infinity."

He took out of the bag another heavy gold coin. "There," said he, "when you find Lafayette, he will need money. Give him *that*. Tell him that it came from Malan, the Jew. No, no; stop. Why should I want my name to go with it? That is selfishness. Yes, yes," he continued, "you may say Malan the Jew sent it. Malan is but a name, but I owe it to my own that you should say a Jew sent it."

He looked into the bag.

"It was Lafayette who said, 'All men are born

9

free and have the right of their birth.' That
means a Jew."

He took another coin out of the bag.

"There, if you ever find Lafayette, he will
need much money. Give him that too. Tell him
the Jew sent it.

He put down another heavy gold coin beside
the bag.

"He said, Lafayette did, that liberty, equality,
and safety were rights of all men."

He took from the bag another coin and placed
it on the table as before. "There, if you ever
find Lafayette, give him that too. He will need
money. Tell him the Jew sent it.

"He said, too, Lafayette did, that no man can
be accused, arrested, or imprisoned, save by just
processes of law. An admirable man is that
same Lafayette. When you see him, give him
that."

He took from the bag another coin.

"He said, the same Lafayette did, that every
man should be regarded as innocent until proven
guilty. You may give him *that*."

The coins were becoming a pile.

"He said, that same noble man, that no person

"Here it is, all of it."

should be disturbed on account of *his religious opinions.* Oh, oh, here it is, all of it."

He poured out the remaining coins on the table.

" Here, let me gather them all up into the bag. Take the bag, gold and all. I could not die content unless I did—— Here, here, if ever you find Lafayette, give him this bag of gold, and it matters not who sent it. Humanity is all one man, and we are children of the same father. I am no stranger to the secret of your Gospel, even if I am a Jew. It is 'He that saveth his own life shall lose it'; one must lose in order to gain, and fall in order to rise, and be broken in order to be made whole. Young travelers, you will find Lafayette. I read it in my soul. There is hidden light there. You will find him."

He gave the bag of gold to young Huger. Would that bag ever find Lafayette?

CHAPTER XVIII.

THE young travelers set out for Olmütz.

Dr. Bollman had entrusted to young Huger another strange secret as they proceeded on their way.

"Are you sure that Lafayette is at Olmütz?" said the American, as they rode along. He had an impression that his companion had not told him all.

"Yes, sure."

"Then you have not told me all?"

"No, but I will do so now."

"Pray tell me without a moment's delay. Have you indeed found Lafayette?"

"I am glad to see that your whole soul is in the question; you will need it—you will need it."

"If you have found Lafayette, I shall henceforth believe in special Providence and in destiny. What is your proof?"

"*I have* found Lafayette, but that may mean struggle for you."

" No matter what it means to me. The heavens are true. If you had not found him, my faith might fall from the sky.

" He is in the dungeon of the Fortress of Olmütz."

"Are you sure? Who told you so?"

" The hospital surgeon."

" What did he say?"

" He said nothing, as I told you before. I said to him that Lafayette was a prisoner there, and that I would deem it a favor if he would give him a pamphlet that contained some notices of two of his friends. He took the pamphlet, as I told you, and said nothing."

" How did he look?"

" His looks told me as much as his tongue could have spoken; as I said, looks speak."

" If he would take a pamphlet to Lafayette, he would take a letter."

" Yes, my good friend, and I prepared one for him. Here is the answer."

" I see. But why did you not tell me this before?"

"I wrote a letter to Lafayette with lime juice, or invisible ink. When he took it to the fire the writing appeared."

"Yes, but how did you send it?"

"By the surgeon."

"But he would suspect a blank piece of paper."

"I had my plan. I wrote the letter in lime juice and took the paper to the surgeon, and in his presence wrote over it a letter in ink, and asked him to take it to Lafayette."

"But how did Lafayette know that the paper contained a writing in invisible ink?"

"That is what I wish you to guess."

"You must have suggested it to Lafayette in the ink letter."

"That would be a delicate matter indeed, but that is what I did. I wrote to him this: 'I am glad of the opportunity of addressing you these words, which, *when read with the usual warmth*, will afford your heart some consolation.'" These were the very words that Bollman wrote, literally translated.

"The next day I met the amiable surgeon. '*I gave the pamphlet to Lafayette*,' he said, 'and he seemed to be much pleased, and wished to know more about one of the friends named in it.'"

They traversed a beautiful country of flax and hemp, shadowed in the distance by the Carpathian hills, and would have been charmed with the sunny valleys had not their daring purpose filled their souls.

"Your hint to Lafayette, in the words 'if you read it with your usual warmth,' seems to me to have been a very slight one on reflection," said Mr. Huger.

"How could you have been bolder and not excited suspicion?" asked his companion. "Lafayette has a very quick mind, and he had received such secret messages before. His very first impulse would be to look for more than appeared on the surface of any letter on political events."

"You are right. He has been trained in that way," said Mr. Huger. "What did you write him in acid?"

"I merely asked him how his friends in Olmütz could see him *secretly*. There was no treason in that."

"No; but the meaning would be clear to a mind like his."

"Of course it would. As clear as the song of Blondel, which Richard helped the Troubadour himself to write. If this plan should succeed, it would be the story of Blondel over again."

"Only this story would be true. We are engaged in no poetry, music, or romance. We may have to pay the forfeit of what we are about to attempt with our lives. What if we should fail?"

"We may fail, but we will tell the civilized world where Lafayette is imprisoned, contrary to the law of nations. Whatever may become of us, *that* alone would be success. Austria cannot hold Lafayette when this fact is known."

"There are two things that impress me in what we are attempting. We are doing an unselfish thing, but we are acting under the laws of the compensations of character. You never saw Lafayette. You have nothing to gain by his release. Why are you doing what you are?"

"Because a perfectly unselfish character draws to itself equally unselfish assistance in the time of trouble. If friends do not help an unselfish man, strangers will. Help is sure to come. There are secret laws of compensation that are his friends, like angels in disguise. This thought gives me faith in God and humanity. If we succeed, what we do will be like a revelation to me. I shall have a vision of God in his laws. And what is the other thing that impresses you?"

"It is the possibility that I, who was almost the first to meet Lafayette when I was a child, should now be imperiling my life to do for him what he did for America. Was my life appointed to this end?"

"I do not know."

"I feel as though an invisible captain was leading me. Whither? No matter. It is duty. He who does right follows an invisible leader and marches with unseen hosts. I have faith, faith, faith! Right-doing is the march of God."

After a journey amid the sunny valleys, they came to Olmütz, whose gloomy castle shadowed the sunrise and sunset air. It was a quiet town now. The army of the Hapsburgs were in other fields, far from the gloomy grandeur of the walled solitude of the Moravia.

CHAPTER XIX.

IN THE INK OF LIFE.

SOON after his arrival in Olmütz, Dr. Bollman called on the surgeon of the military fortress, to resume his discussion of the effects of confinement upon prisoners of state.

"How is the health of Lafayette?" he asked, after a long discussion.

"Long imprisonment has told upon him. It has lost him his hair and shrunk his muscles; he can be now but the shadow of the man he was."

"Is he allowed any exercise?"

"A little—under guard."

The surgeon arose, and took down a pamphlet from a shelf and said:

"Lafayette wished me to return to you this pamphlet with his thanks. It has seemed to exercise a very hopeful influence upon him. I have never seen him so cheerful as he has been since reading it; in his long imprisonment he has been much deprived of the knowledge of the world.

"Is he much restricted here?"

"Yes, yes. When he entered here, he was told that he would not be allowed any communication with the outside world; that his friends should never know where he was, and that he would never be allowed to leave this place."

"What was the excuse for such severity?"

"That the freedom of Lafayette was incompatible with the peace of the royal governments of Europe; that he was a common enemy of monarchy, and should be so treated by the royal powers. For a long time after he came here he had only scanty food, and was allowed few resources but his own reflections.

"I have seen him standing in his damp cell, peering into the sky, whose changes of light and shade were all that he could see. Occasionally a bird flew by. Sometimes a cloud passed with the glow of the sun, which must have looked to him like a heavenly chariot. A bird sometimes came to the bars of the window. When once its song reached him, it must have seemed to tell him of the freedom of a lost world. He has been less restricted

of late.   The interest of America and England in
his welfare has led to his being treated more like
a prisoner of state.

"I have done all I could to make his condition
better and happier, else I should not have taken
to him that pamphlet.   I have recommended that
he be allowed to go out under guard, and it has
been so ordered.   He sometimes is allowed to
ride over the bridges and outside the town into
the open country."

Dr. Bollman put the pamphlet into his pocket,
and returned to the hotel and went to his room.
There he was immediately joined by Huger, who
had been impatiently waiting his return.

"What has happened?" asked the American
student.

"I cannot tell you yet, till I have examined this
pamphlet."

"What pamphlet?"

"The one I sent to Lafayette."

"Has he returned it to you?"

"He has."

"Then it contains invisible writing.   Let us
examine it."

"But how could Lafayette obtain invisible ink?"

"Acid—lime juice."

"He would not be likely to be allowed such a thing in his cell."

"If he took the meaning of the *usual warmth*, the pamphlet somehow and somewhere will communicate to us the fact."

"Look."

The two turned the leaves of the pamphlet, holding them before a strong light.

"I see something there," said the young American.

"So do I."

"It is not written with invisible ink. It is pale printing, as though it was part of the original tablet."

"Like brick dust."

"No, it is not that; it is blood." Read——"

"*My health is poor.*"

"That means nothing. There it is again. Read——"

"*I am allowed to ride out into the forest, under guard.*"

"That means much," said Dr. Bollman. "It means that he has read aright my message. Read it with the *usual warmth.*"

"It means that he may cross the bridge to the wood," said Huger.

"It means that his friends must have force to rescue him," said Dr. Bollman.   "'Under guard,' that means much."

"We cannot secure force."

"We can use wit—invention.   Remember that the Bastille fell."

"We must secure lodgings in the wood."

"And trusty servants."

"And horses."

"I have not the means to procure all we need for such an exploit as this promises to be," said Dr. Bollman.

"But I have—and for the sake of America, you have everything I can command.   For the sake of Washington—all.   For the sake of Yorktown— all.   For the sake of Lafayette, for the heart of Lafayette, which is the heart of liberty, destiny may do with me what it will—he loved others better than himself, and I will love him more than myself.   I have never been so moved before.   I have never felt like this before.   Such an exaltation as possesses me is glory."

"You have, indeed, caught the spirit of your

hero. One light kindles a thousand. You are probably the only man in the world who, at this crisis, could feel all that you feel. We live in spheres of sympathy in this world, and there are a thousand worlds in one. The patriotic have a sphere of their own; they are a noble part of the world."

"And those who struggle for the welfare of all mankind, as has Lafayette, possess the hearts of all true people in the world. Patriotism is good, but the good of mankind is more than any one country, or any single family of nations. My heart says for America, 'Long live Lafayette!' and for France, 'Vive la Lafayette!' and for the world and immortality, 'Onward, O Lafayette, to justice, liberty, and peace!'"

Their windows looked on the bridges. It was the coming on of a still, beautiful evening. Afar the country lay glimmering in the sunset light.

"There is no time to lose," said Dr. Bollman. "Let us seek an inn near the wood, on this very evening, before the gates close."

They went out together. The fortress darkened behind them. They took lodgings near the town, and began to inquire for servants and horses to attend them as travelers. A groom and two horses were procured.

" Do the officers of the fortress often ride out this way ?" they asked the groom.

" Yes, often, and the prisoners of state, under guard."

" Have you here any notable prisoners of state ?"

" I suppose so. We would not know them if there were."

" How do such people ride ?"

"Usually in open carriages with an armed soldier behind them. So I have seen them."

The two students soon made a friend of the groom. They found that he could be intrusted with their plan, and they made him a confidant of it. They would now have three men against three men, and two swift horses.

Their plan was to wait for Lafayette's carriage, to rush out and disarm the guard, frighten the driver, mount Lafayette on the swiftest horse, and point out to him the nearest road to the frontier, while they, too, should mount the other horse and reach the frontier by some other way, so that suspicion might not be aroused.

It was a daring, hazardous plan. But an awakened spirit, fired by an overwhelming motive, does not hesitate. Events march through life toward the height.

Strange, indeed, must have been the feelings of Francis K. Huger in the woods of Olmütz. He had a mother in America, and his thoughts must have turned toward her. She was a noble woman, and must also have felt that her spirit would approve what he was doing and all that he was imperiling.

He was a true Southerner, and amid the grandeur of the old world his heart was still in the Carolinas. The old plantation house by the sea was his home. At Charleston his father had fallen; was he about to honor his State, and its lovely capital, by this exploit in the shadows of the Carpathians and under the Austrian sky?

What matter what followed? He must be that which he had ought to be. We all must be, or be nothing.

10

CHAPTER XX.

PERILOUS.

AT the close of a glowing November afternoon, while yet the sky was a living
splendor, an open carriage passed out
one of the gates of Olmütz, taking the road
toward the open country and the wood. On it
were the driver and two soldiers, and in it was a
worn prisoner of state, once Marquis, but now
Citizen Lafayette.

It was the hour of riding, and carriages were
returning toward the gay city. The sunset
brightened, and the air was still.

Soon two horsemen appeared on horseback, following the carriage at a distance. They excited
no suspicion, for it was a common thing for
people, and especially for visitors and travelers, to
ride on horseback into the open country at that
hour of the day.

The carriage went on for some miles, amid the
lovely landscapes of rural homes and gardens.

The two horsemen followed in the dusty distance, now nearer, now farther away, but never out of sight of the prisoner of state.

The two horsemen were Dr. Eric Bollman and Francis K. Huger. They were engaged in an earnest conversation as they rode along. The heart of each was bounding with excitement. They had sent forward a relay of horses to a public house on the road that led to the confines of Silesia, which were near to Austria, but outside of the emperor's jurisdiction.

" Our plan is as perfect as we could have made it," said Bollman, " and thus far it is working well. I influenced the surgeon to prevail upon the governor to let Lafayette have exercise under guard. My thought has been carried out. I influenced Old Malan the Jew, and I have his purse. That argues success, a Jew's purse, and a purse for Lafayette, whom that Jew never saw."

" I have offered you all that I have," said Huger, wishing to add a good augury to these seemingly fortunate circumstances.

"Yes, and who in all the world could I have secured that would have brought a heart like yours to the cause ? "

"Any true American would have done it," said the student traveler.

"But few Americans would have been able to do it," said Bollman.

"It does look as though fate was with us. An hour will tell."

The two horsemen carried pistols, but the weapons were not loaded. They did not intend to take life.

Their plan followed the suggestion of Lafayette, written in blood. They expected to see the carriage stop, and Lafayette dismount, and walk along the way ; then to rush up to him, to mount him on their swiftest horse, to put into his hand the bag of gold that had been given them by Malan the Jew ; to tell him to ride like the wind toward Silesia; that he would find a relay of horses awaiting on the way, and that they would join him beyond the frontier.

They were not disappointed in the beginning of the unfolding of their plan. Several miles were passed, when the carriage of Lafayette stopped. It was before a wood.

"An advantageous place, that," said Dr. Bollman.

"He is alighting," said Huger. "Just as I have seen it, as it were in a dream."

"Now is our time," said Dr. Bollman.

They spurred their horses.

"In an hour from now Lafayette will be free, or we will be prisoners, or dead."

Lafayette had descended from the carriage and was walking along beside it, but slowly falling behind it.

The sunset light was gleaming over the dark wood. There were few passers in the way.

"I have only one concern about what may happen," said Huger, "it is about my widowed mother. She is a soldier's widow."

"And you are the son of a soldier. See, he is as far behind the carriage as the guard will allow him to be. This is our opportunity. Spurs!"

The two horsemen flew forward, and met Lafayette at the border of the wood.

"You are Lafayette?" said Bollman.

"Yes, Lafayette, and you my friends. What is done, must be done at once."

"The world is seeking you, and we are its messengers. Mount my horse and fly to Silesia," said Bollman. "Halfway between here and

Silesia you will meet our groom with a relay of
horses; then you will be safe. God ride with
you! Fly! You will need money," he added.
" Here is a bag of gold. It comes from Malan, a
Jew in Vienna."

Lafayette attempted to leap upon the horse
when the guard came running up with a drawn
sword.

"Halt! Disarm!" cried Dr. Bollman.

A struggle ensued, when Lafayette was
wounded. But he mounted the horse and swiftly
rode away under the cover of the wood.

Friendly night was coming on. But Lafayette
was a stranger in the place. Which was the road
to Silesia? Which was the road where the groom
and relay of horses were awaiting him?

And now comes the most noble act of young
Huger's life. The two had intended to escape on
the one horse left, which was heavy, but Lafayette had mounted the heavy horse instead of the
light one intended for him.

"That horse cannot carry us both," said
Huger. "Lafayette needs you; take the horse
and flee after him, and leave me to my fate."
These were nearly his own words.

The attempted rescue of Lafayette.

Dr. Bollman hesitated.

"He will be likely to go wrong unless you ride after him. Go! I will hide in the wood. Forget me! Go! whatever happens to me, go!"

Dr. Bollman mounted the horse and rode after Lafayette, but, alas, the prisoner of Olmütz had already taken the wrong way.

Francis Huger was left alone in the wood. He hoped for safety under cover of the night, but the nightfall was slow. He was all alone, and capture seemed certain, and that death.

Presently he heard the great bells of Olmütz clanging, and the signal guns firing. He thought that the guard had returned, and troops of the fortress would soon be flying down the road.

He was right. The dragoons came flying out of the city, sounding the alarm, and calling on the peasants to follow them. In an hour the country was aroused. Men and women were searching everywhere for Lafayette and his would-be rescuers.

Lafayette, who had taken the wrong road, was overtaken and arrested that November evening. He was carried back to the fortress and put in irons. He was deprived of every comfort of life; his wound was painful. A chain was put around his body in such a way that he could scarcely turn over in bed. He was allowed no light, no linen, no word of information from his friends. He was, as it were, buried alive. It was strange that he survived this living tomb.

Dr. Bollman was also captured, cast into prison, and his life made a torture while he awaited his trial.

The peasants had discovered young Huger in the wood early in the evening, and they followed him. He was hounded like a stag. He was compelled to surrender, and was taken back to Olmütz in the shadow of the night, and put into a separate prison in the charge of a merciless keeper.

Deserted by all mankind he passed the hours of his solitary existence. What was the fate of Lafayette? He could not know. Of Bollman? He could ask no questions.

He had one request that he made of the jailor.

"May I send word to my mother in America that I am alive?"

"Silence!"

A dead silence fell upon him. The world as it

were vanished away. For him there was neither sun, moon, nor stars. The rattle of the jailor's keys, and the coming and departure of merciless feet, were all the sounds that broke the chill winter days. He was at last brought to trial, and emerged into the winter light. Bollman was tried with him.

Great events were happening in the world. Napoleon was the master of France, and he had conquered Italy and humiliated Austria. The politics of the world were changing, and Austria and Prussia now trembled before France. There was a ray of hope for the three prisoners in these events.

The widow in her South Carolina home ceased to receive letters from her boy. Had he been waylaid? Was he dead?

The waves moaned on the shore, and in sunlight, moonlight, and starlight, she often turned her eyes thither, and thought of her boy—and perhaps of the midnight consecration of Lafayette.

The immediate attempt to rescue Lafayette failed. Hope must for the moment have died in the two students' hearts. But had it failed? No! The world was to learn by these unhappy events where Lafayette was, and the young, students' efforts were to be the inspiration that led the heart of mankind to set free the Knight of Liberty. The tyranny of tyrants had been discovered, and Austria was to shrink from the responsibility of her unlawful deeds. Right efforts do not fail. Nothing that is right fails. Dungeons stay, but they do not prevent the course of events. Men suffer, they sometimes perish for a noble cause; but the cause wins, and he whose soul loves the cause more than himself has in him the consciousness of victory.

The bells of two worlds were yet to ring for Lafayette; and as for Francis K. Huger, if we were writing a fairy tale we could hardly fancy for him a more happy destiny than was to follow these strange events.

CHAPTER XXI.

THE SECRET WAS OUT.

THE city of Olmütz, the garrison, and the country around, now knew that the prisoner who had been rescued, escaped, and been recaptured was none other than the illustrious Lafayette. The news flew to England, France, and America.

Mme. Lafayette had been a prisoner in the south of France. Most of her near relatives and friends had fallen under the guillotine; the estates of Lafayette had been for the time confiscated, and this true wife and mother had suffered all the distresses of the times of the Black Cockade.

But emerging from prison to see again the light of the sun, and to breathe the fresh air of the fields, there came to her the thrilling news that the prison of Lafayette had been found.

Her health was broken and her strength wasted by imprisonment. But she could say, " This is the news for which I have been praying in lonely places and solitary hours. I will go to the court of Austria and plead for my husband, and, if I cannot gain his release, I will beg to share his prison with him."

Such, in substance, was the declaration of this most heroic woman. With her two daughters, she traveled to Vienna and gained an audience with the emperor, Francis I. The emperor received her coldly. He did not wish to grant her requests, but public opinion compelled him to consider the petition of this helpless woman. To her pleading she received this hard and final answer from a state minister:

"You may visit your husband at Olmütz, but you must carry nothing to him and never expect to leave the prison alive."

She heard the decision with a lofty spirit.

"Do you accept the permission under these conditions?" asked the minister.

"I do."

Such was the wife of Lafayette.

One day the cell of the hero was opened, and cries of joy rent the damp and dismal air. Before Lafayette stood his wife, from whom he had not heard for three years, and his daughters whom he would hardly have known had they not come with their mother.

"My wife, my dear wife, what has brought you here ?"

"My heart and my prayers," she might have answered. But she told him she had come to share his prison and his fate. Says a friend of Lafayette : "That meeting cannot be imagined or described ; the prison wall rang with a joy that had never been heard there before."

The two daughters, one aged sixteen and one aged thirteen, were placed in separate cells. They had committed no crime, but such was despotism.

Mme. Lafayette, after a year's imprisonment, grew so feeble in health that it was thought that she must be released or soon die.

She petitioned for the temporary release of herself and daughters, and waited an answer. It came :

"You may be released, but on the condition that you shall never see your husband again."

"Go," said Lafayette, "go for the sake of your health and your children. Do not think of me. Go !"

"My dear husband, I would rather die with you here in prison than to live in our beautiful country of Lagrange without you."

But Napoleon, who had conquered Italy, now dictated terms of treaty to humiliate Austria. One of these terms was that Austria should set free all the state prisoners of France. Lafayette was among the number, and he went forth again into the great world of the sun and flowers, taking the faithful hearts of his family with him.

And Huger and Bollman? Long before this the influence of the political changes in Europe had caused them to be set free.

Dr. Bollman became an eminent physician, but he never saw Lafayette again after the scene of the encounter in the wood. But Mme. Lafayette wrote him a most affecting letter, a part of which I quote. Some of my readers will like to read it.

LETTER FROM MME. LAFAYETTE TO DR. BOLLMAN.

"OLMÜTZ, May 22, 1796.

"I am at last enabled to write to you, and to express to you all the sentiments with which we are so deeply affected. The first wish of my heart is to assure you of our gratitude. I am likewise eager to express my regret for having been unable

to address you sooner. In the prisons of Paris
I had been informed of your generous under-
taking, and I was aware that you and M. Huger
were in custody ; but we had been, and were still
in France, exposed to such tyrannical oppression—
such efforts were made to annihilate the recol-
lection of one whose principles and whose example brought to mind the duty of resistance to that
oppression, and terror had so completely paralyzed
every heart, that it was impossible, especially in
my personal position, to obtain many details
respecting M. Lafayette and yourself. Besides,
I was myself overwhelmed by the most appalling
calamities that can be inflicted on the heart of
a daughter and a sister, and I felt the necessity of
coming to this place, in order to regain a portion
of my faculties and to recover my strength.

"I at length obtained a passport for the United
States, and an American vessel conveyed me to
Hamburg, whence I ought to have written to
you ; but as I had received in that city only an
imperfect account of all that referred to you ; as
I was, moreover, persuaded by what I heard at
Vienna that I could easily correspond from this
place, and, as I confess that myself and my
daughters were completely taken up with the idea
of arriving here, we thought that the expression
of our sensibility would be more agreeable to you

in the name of all four; and you may easily
imagine that, from the first moment of our
meeting, we had to satisfy the eager impatience
of M. Lafayette to hear of you. From him we
learned, with intense interest and admiration, all
the circumstances which we had previously known
but in part. We were informed of all that you
had done in Russia; we were aware of the time,
the efforts, and the address, which it must have
cost you at Olmütz to correspond with him; we
were apprised of your courageous attempt, but we
were ignorant of the generosity with which you
adopted Lafayette's idea, and the zeal with which
you facilitated his flight, when every mode of
serving him at Vienna was exhausted. It is
impossible for me to describe to you how much
we were affected by all the details of that day, on
which you and M. Huger displayed such intre-
pidity, such delicacy, such indifference to your
own personal safety, and such undivided devotion
to the idea of saving the man who spoke to us of
your efforts with such well-merited enthusiasm.
He would fain himself explain to you how, after
stopping on the road, in spite of what you had
told him, to see you on horseback; obliged afterward to walk, because the blood and filth with
which he was covered attracted attention; having
stopped again, and even, in his uneasiness for

both of you, having for a moment retraced his
steps, he was forced to return to Sternberg; and
how, having reason to believe that you had proceeded across the fields, he endeavored to over-
take you before your arrival in that place, although he suffered severely from his first fall;
how, in a word, being unacquainted with the
name of Hoff, and not knowing the direct road to
Silesia, by which he had arrived in a carriage, and
being unable to ask many questions without ex-
citing observation, especially on account of the
singularity of his appearance, he was in the end
arrested. He then, at least, had the momentary
consolation of believing that you had both
escaped; for it was only at Olmütz that he heard
of M. Huger's arrest, and he was not certain even
of yours till he underwent the interrogatory to
which, through consideration for both of you, he
consented to reply; and in the course of which,
having refused to speak on the secret correspond-
ence, it was found necessary to prove to him that
the surgeon and yourself had disclosed everything.
I shall make no effort to describe to you his feelings during your horrible captivity. Though we
found him recovered, especially since he had been
informed of your deliverance, it was but too evi-
dent how much his heart had suffered from the
moral tortures so basely inflicted on him—tortures

11

which even to me, who had been in France, the
witness and the victim of the most atrocious and
tyrannical anarchy, appeared the most cruel refinement of barbarity that hatred could contrive.

.   .   .   .

"You would render us a vast additional service
if you could transmit to the excellent and generous M. Huger the expression of our gratitude,
admiration, and regard, and the assurance of the
feelings with which Lafayette is inspired by the
idea of owing the highest possible obligation to
the son of the first man who received him, and of
the first friend whom he possessed, in America.
Will you have the kindness to undertake to speak
to M. Pinckney, of our grateful attachment to
him, and also of our confidence, and to say a
thousand kind things to our charming friend, Mrs.
Church? We are too well assured of her husband's friendship not to feel assured that he too is
wholly occupied with our affairs.

"Adieu, Sir; when shall we be able to speak to
you in person of the feelings which we so justly
entertain toward you, and of which our hearts
must forever be so deeply sensible?

"NOAILLES LAFAYETTE."

CHAPTER XXII.

THE KEY OF THE BASTILLE.

WHAT shall be done with George?" So asked Mme. Lafayette of her daughters, when she first resolved to go in search of her husband. George was her son, then a boy.

"I shall take you with me; but George Washington, the heart of his father, what shall we do with him?"

"Let me go with you," said the boy.

"There is one heart in the world to whom I can trust you. It is that of Washington. He will be true to you for your father's sake. You bear his name. I will send you to him."

A Boston gentleman was about to sail for America, whom Mme. Lafayette knew, and of whose character she had a high opinion.

"May I trust my boy to you?" she asked of him. "Will you direct him to Washington? He

will tell his own story to Washington when he
meets the statesman."

"You may trust him to me, to Washington, and
to the American public. Everyone in America
will be a brother to the son of Lafayette. Washington will be a father to him."

"If my husband should ever gain his freedom,
he will ever love those who befriend his boy, at
this time of dire distress and peril. As I said, sir,
that boy is the heart of his father. Their lives
are one. I know that Washington will be a
father to him. I can trust the great American,
and I can trust America!"

Some families have noble and beautiful friend-
ships, and the relation between Lafayette and his
son made both lives happy. Lafayette gave his
son the name of George Washington, as a seal of
eternal friendship for the hero of the West. As
the boy grew up, they became companions, they
loved each other, and each seemed to be happy
when the other was near.

Lafayette trained this boy to republican principles, he taught him that wealth and fame were of
themselves of little worth, and that character is
everything.

The boy accepted these teachings; he believed them; they entered into his heart.

An intimate friend of Lafayette's thus pictures the conclusions to which that hero came, after his study of men:

" Proud of having lost his feudal nobility, Lafayette looked upon the land of liberty as giving a promise to mankind of a richer harvest of public virtue than the barren fields of sable, gold, or azure, so long moistened with the tears and the blood of nations. He recognized no other nobility than that of the feelings of the soul; he admitted no other distinctions among men than those acquired by them from their virtues, their talents, or their services to their fellow-men.

" The aristocracy of money, that of the rich man, is one of the most powerful, one of those which in general excite the strongest desire to form part of it. To become wealthy, and consequently to possess the power and means of satisfying one's tastes and passions, is to many the object of existence. Nevertheless, the aristocracy of money may have something noble in it, when, like the horn of plenty, it bestows its treasures on men whom it relieves, on commerce which it animates, or on the earth which it fertilizes,—but what is it in itself? It frequently requires little

intelligence to amass much money, supposing it
legitimately acquired; but great qualities are
required to make a prudent use of wealth, and to
circulate it freely, without extravagance. The
prodigal sow their treasures in the bed of a tor-
rent, without honor to themselves, and without
advantage to their country. On the other hand,
the avaricious capitalist impoverishes his country,
by hoarding wealth and by stopping the circu-
lation of the vivifying metal. Like the strong
box, he possesses a value only when full, and is of
use only when he can be emptied. Avarice is the
rust of the soul: nothing grand or generous can
germ or develop itself in the miser's withered
heart!

"The pride arising from the possession of
wealth is always ridiculous: it can make a fool
of a man estimable in other respects, by causing
him to forget or to conceal his origin, which no
other person forgets, and which malice delights in
exposing to public view; by urging him to make
an ostentatious display of the weakness which he
ought to conceal; and especially, by filling him
with absurd pretensions to the other descriptions
of aristocracy.

"The *aristocracy of intelligence*, undoubtedly
renders highly commendable the men who confer
honor on their country, or contribute to the wel-

fare of mankind, by their labors in literature, science, or the arts ; but in what estimation would a literary man, an artist, or a man of science be held, if his character were found unworthy of his talent, or of his intellectual superiority?"

Such were Lafayette's views of life, and these opinions became a part of the heart and character of his son. Lafayette himself says of his boy :

"The fact is, that George, who is a republican patriot,—and I have met with few such in my lifetime,—has besides a passion for the military profession, for which I think him adapted as he possesses a sound and calm judgment, a just perception, a strong local memory, and will be equally beloved by his superiors, his comrades, and his subordinates. I love him with too much tenderness to make any distinction between his desires and mine ; and I am too great an enemy to oppression of every description to place a restraint on the wishes of a beloved son, nearly twenty years of age. I could joyfully see him covered with honorable scars, but beyond that supposition, I have not the courage to contemplate existence."

The son of Lafayette, with a tutor named Frestel, landed in Boston in August, 1785. He

desired seclusion, and he passed by the name of
Motier; his full name was George Washington
Motier de Lafayette.

The boy and his tutor had come to Boston on
the invitation of a man named Cabot, who com-
municated the arrival of the son of Lafayette
to President Washington, then at Philadelphia.
Washington answered, " I will be to him a father
and friend, protector and supporter."   .

Washington met the boy at Philadelphia, and
the latter and his tutor made their home with
him there.   They went later to Mount Vernon.

It was a still, clear day, as the boy approached
the simple republican house, with its great portico
and grand trees.

On the same eventful year that the Bastille fell,
Washington had been made by the people the
President of the great Republic of the West that
Lafayette had done so much to found.   He was
now about to retire from the Presidency, and was
already preparing to make Mount Vernon his
permanent home.   His farewell address had gone
forth to the American people.

When Lafayette was compelled to flee to
Flanders, he was the commander of the victorious

army of Ardennes. It was the slanders of the Jacobins, who accused him of treason, that began the series of events that drove him out of France.

As Washington and the son of his old friend came to the mansion, at Mount Vernon, the boy stood under the portico and looked out on the Potomac, that lay like a glimmer of silver among the clouds of trees. The estate was not like Lagrange, his own home. Everything in the new country seemed strange to him.

Lady Washington did her best to make the boy happy on this serene day. Her sympathy was that of a mother.

"My son, you are welcome here to our hearts and home," we may suppose her to have said.

"You have a home, but my father is an exile and a prisoner, if indeed he be alive," said the boy in his heart.

"You bear our name," we fancy her to have said. "Your father not only honored our nation when he gave you that name, but he implied in it that you were to be a son to us. You are our son, and the nation's son, and here is to be your home, until your father returns."

"Returns, from where? I do not know where

my father is. They say that an American young
man has discovered him at Olmütz. My
mother and sisters have gone there." He looked
down the green banks, through the oaks and magnolias. His heart was at Lagrange, or with his
father in the Austrian prison.

"Lady Washington?"

"My son."

"You have a happy home. Washington fought
for liberty, and I am an exile in the country for
which he fought."

One of the family at Mount Vernon came out
on the portico, holding in his hand a great key.

"You are the son of Lafayette?" asked the
gentleman.

"Yes, my father is Lafayette."

"His heart sought us in our distress as a
nation, and the heart of the nation will always
love his son."

"But he has lost all, in trying to gain the liberties of France. Oh, my poor father! my poor
mother!"

"The General of the Army of Ardennes has
not lost all. The times have changed, my boy;
but France will one day become a free nation, like

America. Your father was a Knight of Liberty to us, he will prove some day to have been the apostle of Liberty to France."

The boy burst into tears.

"My father, my father! What did he not do for France? I wish that I might enfold him in my arms, as I used to do. I long for him all the time. I used to feel his heart beat,—that heart, that heart,—I wish that I might feel it again. Do you think that France will ever again love my father?"

"My boy, do you know what that is?"

The gentleman held up before him the key of the Bastille.

"No, sir. It is an old key, but I never saw it before."

"Your father sent it to us."

"My father! Let me take it."

"Your father wrote this letter to Washington, when he sent the key."

He handed the boy the letter. It read:

"Give me leave, my dear General, to present to you a picture of the Bastille, just as it looked a few days after I ordered its demolition, with the main key of the fortress of despotism.

"It is a tribute which I owe, as a son to my adopted father, as an aid-de-camp to my general, as a missionary of liberty to its patriarch."

The boy took the key and kissed it.

"My father sent it?"

"Yes, my boy. That was the key of the Bastille. That key will never unlock the Bastille again."

"No, sir."

"And there will never be another bastille in France after what your father has done."

"Do you think that France will be a free nation like yours?"

"Yes, my son; you hold in your hand the key of the Bastille, and when the Bastille fell, despotism fell. Your father has made France free, and her people will never again be slaves. Be happy with us; you bear our name. This home shall be your own. The nation will love you until your father returns. You should be a proud boy. Your father's sword helped to make this nation free, and you hold in your hand the key of the Bastille."

George Washington Lafayette would have been delighted in the new country had his father been with him.

Soon after Washington left the chair of state (March 4, 1797), he proceeded to Alexandria. It was beautiful weather. The hills, valleys, and river banks were filled with flowers. Bird songs enlivened the bright air. The children strewed the streets with flowers as he passed, and Cincinnatus-like, the great commoner went back to the farm and people, amid the almost universal praise of mankind.

The boy saw the glory of the noble man. He heard the applause of the people, and he was proud that his own name entered into this great expression of gratitude — George Washington Lafayette.

He looked up to Washington, that serene man, and wondered and dreamed. Did this man ever know sorrow? Had he ever been maligned, as had been his father?

One day, as he was sitting on the great piazza of Mount Vernon, overlooking the green, the woods, and the river, he said to a gentleman, the one of the family who had handed him the key:

"Did anyone ever think evil or speak a hard word of Washington?"

"My boy," said the gentleman, "read that."

He handed the boy a paper called *The Aurora*.
The boy read:

"If ever a nation has been debauched by a
man, the American nation has been by Washington. If ever a nation has been deceived by a
man, the American nation has been by Washington. Let his conduct then be an example to
future ages. Let it serve to be a warning that no
man may ever be an idol. Let the history of the
Federal Government instruct mankind, that the
masque of patriotism may be worn to conceal the
foulest designs against the liberties of a people."

The boy read this, and more like it, with aston-
ishment.

"They destroyed my father's influence in that
way," he said. "Can it be, can it be? Is there
no help for such slanders as these?"

"Yes, my boy."

"What, sir?"

"Time. Time tells the truth about all men.
When a mean man injures another, it creates
a sympathy for him in the heart of some noble
man, and so he who is unjustly treated gains
more than he loses. My boy, I have something

wonderful to tell you. But I will let another bear the news."

Lady Washington sent out to the boy a letter. He read it with surprise and wet eyes, and said:

" His name is Huger."

" Whose name ? "

" The young American, who found where my father was imprisoned."

" Did you know that Huger was the first boy your father met on landing on the American shore ? "

" No, sir ; no."

" He was ; and he took him upon his knee, and loved him at once, and the two became friends. That boy then could not have been more than three or four years of age." He added: " My boy, what did I just say to you ? Listen to it again. When a mean man injures another, it creates a sympathy for him in the heart of some good man, and so he who is unjustly treated gains more than he loses. Is not this likely to be true of your father? The laws of God are good, and they make Time a friend to all."

CHAPTER XXIII.

THE BAG OF GOLD AGAIN.

APTURED," said Malan, the Jew, as he paced his garden, after the news of the capture of Lafayette had been brought by courier to Vienna. "And where is my bag of gold?"

"Any injury that we do to another, hurts our own souls," he continued, pacing to and fro under the lime trees. "And any good that we do for another helps our own souls." He paused and looked down the green sward.

"But where is my bag of gold? The governor of the fortress has got it. It has gone to enrich *him*."

The parrot saw that her master was in trouble, and began to make inquiries. "What is the matter, Polly?" was a common expression with her, and she was saying it over and over, in English, and old Malan understood English well.

The Jew turned his face toward the sky, which

was suffused with sunset light. The good spirit in his soul had been growing for years, and it now brought beautiful thoughts to him.

"Any injury that we seek to do others harms our own souls," he said, and then, with a beneficent face, he added: "And any good which we seek to do for another helps our own souls. Where is my bag of gold? It is in my soul. It will bless my soul, but I wish it were in Lafayette's pocket."

"What's the matter?" asked the blue-fronted bird.

"Nothing is the matter, you poor, simple, beautiful creature. To him who does right everything in this world is right, and it will all be well in the world to come. Good desires are the soul of events, and I have the wish that before I die I may take the hand of Lafayette; I would make a pilgrimage to meet him; the many make the nation, but a few sympathetic hearts the family of God."

The children gathered around the old man under the lime tree. "Hurrah!" said the Bolivar parrot. "Hurrah for *Lafayette!*"

"That will never do," said the Jew. He covered the bird's cage with a mantle, and with poor

12

Polly it was night. That was a dangerous word now, a very dangerous word. It haunted his thoughts. Were a single watchman or guard to hear it, it would bring him under suspicion.

"And now, children, you may go," he said pleasantly, and led them toward the gate.

He closed the gate and removed the cage from the lime tree to his room, and there sat down to dream of liberty in the land of the fame of Washington, and of the triumphs of human rights in the West.

"All the world is one country," he said in his proverbial way; "and there was never a cause that lacked a Curtius."

There came a heavy rap on the door.

The Jew started and listened. It was repeated. He went to the door, and found there an Austrian officer.

"I wish to speak with you," said the officer.

"Come in."

The officer entered.

"Did you exchange money for a young American traveler, a week or more ago?"

"I did."

"That man has been arrested."

"That were no fault of mine."

"He was engaged in a conspiracy to liberate a prisoner of state. He was rich, for there was found on the prisoner of state a treasure which only a rich man could have furnished him."

"And please you, what might it have been?"

"It was a bag of gold."

There was another loud rap on the door. Another officer entered.

"I have traced the case here," said the first officer. "We must investigate."

"There is no need," said the second.

"Why?"

"Do you not see that the man is a Jew?"

"Yes; but he confesses that he exchanged money for the young man."

"That is nothing; he did not give the young man the treasure."

"Why not?"

"Why not? Was it ever heard that a Jew gave one, not his countryman, a bag of gold?"

The officer rose. The parrot had put her pretty head out from under the mantle.

"Hurrah!"

The Jew trembled. But the two officers went

away laughing good humoredly. Their feet echoed along the street, farther and farther away.

The old Jew's heart was hurt. He thought of the reproachful taunt: " Did ever a Jew?"

" Did ever a Jew?" he said. "Yes, for liberty; yes, for humanity; yes, for God! My days are swifter than a weaver's shuttle, but I shall live. The gray hairs in my beard are numbering my hours, but I am not yet altogether gray. I shall meet Lafayette some day, if he lives, and then will come back to me my bag of gold. ' Did ever a Jew?' Yes—Malan."

He sank upon the couch. The lights went out in the streets, and the candle failed in the room. He dreamed of a happier day for his and every race, and his heart was light, for he had contributed to that day—" Did ever a Jew?"—a bag of gold.

CHAPTER XXIV.

FATHER AND SON.

LAFAYETTE'S son returned to France and entered the army. It was Lafayette's pride to watch the development of this boy; whatever might happen to himself, he desired the happiness of him whose life to him was more than his own. But in this youth, as in the case of the ancient patriarch, his character was to be tested, and his faith tried.

Napoleon was rising in military glory. He had eclipsed Lafayette and become the popular hero of France. He followed his great ambitions, and instead of losing himself in a cause he lost his cause in himself.

After Lafayette had declined to support him as consul for life, Napoleon became the secret enemy of the great apostle of liberty. He once offered him a position of the value of twice his then diminished income, but Lafayette would not be untrue to the principles he had proclaimed in his declaration of the rights of man and in the constitution, for money.

George Washington Lafayette entered the army under Napoleon. His high character and bravery as a young officer won him distinction. Napoleon could not bend Lafayette, but he could disappoint him in his son, and this he seems to have resolved to do.

One day this son returned to his father with a face of grief.

"You have not been promoted," said Lafayette. "It is no fault of your own; it is on my account; you are suffering for your father's honor. I am sorry that it is so, but I must be what I ought to be. What new humiliation brings you here, for I see that your heart is hurt?"

"General Grouchy desires my resignation," said the young man. "He can give no true reason for it; I think it is because Napoleon wishes it so. I have done my duty and been a true soldier. I have obeyed, dared, and sought the most perilous service."

"Were Napoleon a magnanimous man he would never belittle himself by treating you thus. An

officer who would treat another in this way has
none of the high qualties of soul that merit glory
—mark my words : Napoleon will fall. Only
what is true lasts, and he that saveth his life shall
lose it.

> " '*Mi!* ça ira, ça ira, ça ira,
> The exalted shall be abased ! '

"I have read the ambition of this man's heart;
he seeks the glory of France for his own glory,
and not for liberty, justice, and the welfare of
mankind. I may hope it is not so ; but from
his own conversations with me, so I fear it is. If
it be so, he will fall. Heaven holds the scales."

" But what can I do ? Shall I resign as he desires? My heart says no ! Resign without a
cause, in the presence of the enemies of France ?
It would be dishonor ! "

"No, my son ; serve France. You may not be
promoted, but in the presence of the enemies of
France, serve the cause. We must wait events
for justice. Time is the friend of all true hearts
and right efforts.

"If I misunderstand Napoleon, time will correct
me. If he be led by ambition, the end will jus-

tify my judgment. I am sorry that you must suffer for my convictions. Serve the cause, and wait."

" I am glad to suffer for your honor. I believe that Yorktown stands for more than all the victories of Napoleon. But I must be a true soldier and obey!"

" Yes, my son ; that is right."

The humiliation of this favorite son made the heart of Lafayette bleed. It was the most cruel experience that could come into his life. But he was proud to know that his boy was a hero. Nothing is lost while honor is gained.

Should Napoleon fall, would Lafayette be magnanimous to him after a refinement of cruelty like this? Events are hastening, and we shall see.

Napoleon became the apparent master of Europe. In 1804 he crowned himself emperor in the Church of Notre Dame, in Paris, and France acclaimed. There was so much that was noble in the life of Napoleon, so many things to be commended, that Lafayette could not be sure that the view that he had taken of him was true, but he knew that to crumble is the fate of all selfish gravitation.   He could be loyal to France and wait.

The emperor went forth to new conquests.   He crowned his brother Joseph, King of Spain.   He rewarded those who were faithful to him with the honors and spoils of the world's battlefields.   He met with reverses, but he rose again.

CHAPTER XXV.

SUNSET AT WATERLOO.

IT was the night of the 17th of June, 1815. There were gay gatherings in Brussels, then a beautiful city, and now one of the most beautiful cities in all the world. The people did not know that Napoleon was rushing forward his fiery and veteran army, of nearly one hundred thousand men, to crush Wellington before the latter could unite his forces with those of the allies against France.

So it was a gay night. The English officers were there, and there were balls at the Hotel de Ville, whose ballroom is still shown, and at other places, and the Duchess of Brunswick had invited Wellington to the festivities of her house, which is now partly or wholly gone.

> " There was a sound of revelry by night,
> And Belgium's capital had gathered then
> Her beauty and her chivalry, and bright
> The lamps shone o'er fair women and brave men.

A thousand hearts beat happily and when
Music arose with its voluptuous swell,
Soft eyes looked love to eyes that spake again.
And all went happy as a marriage bell."

The city blazed. But amid the festival, there was heard the roar of cannon afar :

" Within a windowed niche of that high hall
Sat Brunswick's fated chieftain ; he did hear
The sound the first amid the festival."

The alarm ended the joyous scenes. Was Napoleon indeed approaching ? Napoleon, who had said that destiny and he were one ? Napoleon, who at the height of his power had once declared that he would ascend to the dictatorship of the world ; that there must be one coinage and one court of appeal for all Europe; that the states of Europe must be melted into one nation, and Paris be the capital ? " Man proposes, but God disposes," an humble Russian woman is reported to have said to him. " I propose and dispose," was the answer. Napoleon struck, but the blow rebounded. But he was again free; and the old guard and young France were following him. He had believed that Providence was on the side of the heaviest artillery, and, if he were indeed approaching, he had the heaviest artillery. Was it the thunder of those guns that were sullenly shaking the halls?

But there was another thunder that was shaking the sky. Black clouds had gathered on the morning of the 18th. The battle of Waterloo was first fought, as it were, in the sky. The artillery of Heaven poured down a deluging rain all that hot, fireless morning, and it made the great plain a sea of mud, over which the heavy artillery of Napoleon would find it hard to pass.

The field of Waterloo is some twelve miles from Brussels. One may ride to it now on the long summer days, and listen to a lecture from the top of the great monumental mole, on which rests the bronze lion of Waterloo, made of French cannon, and return to the city at night, through the lovely forests and wide poppy-dotted gardens.

Terror filled the city as the army formed to hurry outward under the clouded stars:

> " And there was mounting in hot haste, the steed,
> The mustering squadron, and the clattering car
> Went pouring forward with impetuous speed,
> And swiftly forming in the ranks of war."

The army swept down through the forest of Ardennes that wet morn :

> " And Ardennes waves above them her green leaves
> Dewy with nature's tear drops as they pass."

The powers that were to decide the fate of Europe were gathering under the clouded sky. "Waterloo was not a battle," says Victor Hugo, " but the change of front of the universe."

Wellington was at a disadvantage, but Blücher, now at a distance, had promised to re-enforce him an hour after noon of that day. Would he come? He had made the promise when he knew not the events that were impending. Napoleon had from 70,000 to 90,000 men, and the Anglo-Netherlands army, or the allies under Wellington, would, should Blücher come, number nearly 70,000, of which 25,000 were British troops.

Should Wellington face the fiery French army, and risk the coming of Blücher? The French had 240 cannon, and he but 156. This he could not have known, and had he known it, he probably did not believe that Providence sided with the heaviest artillery.

Napoleon was certain of victory as he stood on

the hills under the lowering sky, and saw his advantage over his foe. He laughed in derision as he sat with his officers, like Xerxes at Salamis.

The green earth was mud; the sky was lead; the skirmish lines blazed and rattled, and between eleven and twelve o'clock the battle began, Napoleon attempting to take Hougoumont, whose well and ruins may still be seen, and into whose well, it is claimed, hundreds of bodies were thrown after the battle, some dead, some wounded, and the wounded crying out piteously, in their open tomb, for hours and days, for rescue and the chance for life. "Had Napoleon taken Hougoumont," says one, "he might have had the world." But Hougoumont was not taken. In its green gardens and orchards, that day, some three thousand men fell. But the men stationed there were heroes, and they felt that to them had been given the key of the temple of fate.

As one visits the ruined château now under the blue sky of summer, amid the gay poppy fields, and hears the birds singing in the cool trees, one can hardly imagine how gray and red and blasting was that day. The low clouds lifted, but the sky was still overcast.

At two o'clock Napoleon felt that the crisis of the battle had come. He did not doubt that " he and destiny were one." Never was Marshal Ney, " the bravest of the brave," prouder than at that hour. He swept down 20,000 men upon Wellington's squares. But the English met the shock with the steadiness of men whose commissions were in their souls. The French met an awful loss.

Did a doubt begin to enter Napoleon's mind now? He had sat on his white steed on the green heights, with his telescope in hand, on that morning of destiny, arrayed like a conqueror whose victory was already assured. His cloak, indeed, concealed his epaulettes, red ribbon, and stars. His white horse had housings of purple velvet, with decorations of N's and eagles. By his side was the victorious sword of Marengo.

Four o'clock came. The great plain and sloping hills were covered with the dead and dying.

The Prince of Orange, who commanded the center, had given his immortal order to the Belgians :

" Never yield an inch."

The army of Wellington had stretched from

château of Hougoumont to a distant farm house called La Haye Sainte.

Wellington sat, mounted on his horse, in front of the old mill of Mount St. Jean, near an elm tree, the site of which is still shown. His aid-de-camp fell by his side, and his officers around him, but his mind never wavered from the fate of the day. A shell came screaming through the air and bursted near him.

" My Lord," said Lord Hill, " what orders do you leave for us if you are killed ?"

" Do as I am doing now."

Seeing that events looked dark, and that Blücher had not come, he said, " Boys, can you think of giving way—remember old England !"

The English moved back behind a ridge, to consolidate.

The army, except the artillery and sharp-shooters, seemed to have disappeared.

Then, if ever, the heart of Napoleon swelled with pride. The dream of his life seemed about to be realized.

" It is the beginning of retreat !" he cried.

" It is a pretty chess board," he had said of the armies in the morning, and the game seemed to have been won. And now was the time to send the glad news to Paris. How the city would blaze with light !

" Fly," said he, to the courier, "and tell them the field is won ! The English are in retreat !"

There remained one thing to be done. It was to sweep Wellington's hidden squares from the plateau. The cavalry must do this and the cavalry were giant men on giant horses. He gazed at the ridge. How splendidly these giants would mount it and hurl their irresistible force down on the other side.

He had by his side a guide named Lacoste. He bent low and said to him, "Is there any obstruction between us and the plateau ?"

The peasant shook his head.

It was not true.

The reader may never have seen a sunken road. If he visit the field of Waterloo to-day he will probably ride through one, for such a road lies between the railway and the mound of the lion.

A sunken road is a deep depression in the centre of a hill. One might pass close to the hill, or even along its side and not know that such a road was there.

13

There was such a sunken road in the ridge between the cavalry and the plateau, and the peasant guide probably knew that there was. But his denial followed his heart and not his conscience.

The grand cavalry charge, in the view of Napoleon, would end all. Then he would sweep toward the center of the continent, and who should stay his eagles? He would be Alexander! He would be Cæsar! France should be the world!

The giant horsemen were three thousand five hundred in number.

How magnificent they looked as their horses mounted the ridge of the plateau!

There were twenty-six squadrons, and eleven hundred and ninety-six sabers and nearly as many lances gleamed in the dissolving air. Ney was at their head, "the bravest of the brave." He drew his saber. They raised their sabers and gave their standards to the air. They moved as one spirit, and if ever victory seemed to hover in the air—victory complete—it was then.

Behind the crest of the plateau, in which was the sunken road, Wellington had consolidated his squares, and he calmly awaited the coming of the army of death.

There was a silence there, and the rush of the three thousand horses seemed to rend the air before the hills. The cuirassiers mounted the ridge. What a scene was there that made the blood fly from each leader's cheek and his heart sink?

There yawned under their very feet the sunken road; a chasm, a grave. They could not halt. Into that chasm the first rank of men and horses went down, then the second rank, crushing their riders, and at last when the road was full of the dead and dying, the rest of the cavalry, impelled by an irresistible momentum, rode over their bodies to new slaughters in the open field.

Two thousand horses and fifteen hundred men were buried, according to the local tradition, in or about this awful abyss, on the following days.

The battle that followed is one of the most terrible in history. Division after division of the English army was borne down, yet the army, as a whole, did what the Iron Duke did, stood like statues.

Ney had four horses shot under him. The

giant horses at times leaped upon the English bayonets. After twelve assaults the English army still stood, and the giant cavalry had spent its force.

Ney sent a message to Napoleon—how it must have shaken the emperor's heart!

"Send me infantry." .

"Infantry!" said Napoleon; "does he think that I can make them?"

Five o'clock came. Wellington looked at his watch.

"It is Blücher or night," he said—meaning help or defeat.

Blücher's army had been delayed by the mud. But early in the battle, under the dissolving clouds, Napoleon had seen a cloud a long way off on the hills that raised his apprehension. He peered through his glass.

"I see a cloud over there," he said. "It looks like troops."

He looked again.

"Soult, what do you see?"

"Men, sire; four or five thousand of them."

"They are columns halting," said one officer.

"They are only trees," said others.

It was now near nightfall. The great cavalry charge had failed; and Blücher was thundering down to the field. To Wellington it was Blücher, and to Napoleon night.

The French reeled back before the third army. At first all was terror and confusion; then the retreat became a rout. "God disposes!"

It was evening. The clouds rolled away. The sky burned. It was sunset.

It was sunset with thee, Napoleon! It was sunset, let us hope, with wars of ambition and conquest in Europe.

But where now is Marshal Ney, the bravest of the brave? He finds a horse, a strange horse, and he mounts it, without hat or sword, and hastens to order back the flying army. But they still fly, shouting, "Long live Marshal Ney."

And Napoleon? He too rides after the fugitives, but they still fly, crying out "Long live the Emperor!"

That June night the moon came out, and under it the battlefield blazed and smoked; and men groaned and died. Nearly fifty thousand men lay on the field.

Napoleon turned toward Paris—what must have

been his thoughts of God, fate, and this change-
able world, in this solitary hour ?

He at first rode alone, but was recognized by
flying men by his gray overcoat and white horse.

There was a great orchard on the farm of
La Belle Alliance. He came to it, and reined his
horse into the shadows. It was a silent place,
dark with leaves. It was there that must have
come to him the full revelation of his fall. Few
things are more pathetic in his history than this
brief night solitude in the lonely orchard.

" What would father say if he saw us now ? " he
had asked of his favorite brother, Joseph, as they
dressed for his coronation in 1804.

His thoughts may have turned to his brother in
this dreadful hour ; he wrote to him a short time
later. Alas! what would his father have said could
he have seen him in the shadows of the French
farmhouse, for that little time alone ? What is
there in history more pathetic than Napoleon in
that orchard of La Belle Alliance, all alone ?

Two French soldiers presently came riding by.
They had lost their way. They discovered him
there in solitude and called after him. Thinking
that call was a warning that he was being pur-

sued, he darted forward, and came to Charleroi. He obtained a post carriage and rode like the wind to the walls of Phillipeville, where he wrote that letter to his brother Joseph. Sleep? did he sleep that night?

And this was the end of the slaughters of men for glory! He went to Paris, and the Assembly demanded his abdication. He must now flee. Where? Whither?

In the midst of his confusion and peril, there came to him a message. Its magnanimity revealed to him a grand man, whose life had been governed by the divinity within. It said in substance, "I will prepare the way for you to go to America."

America? Whence came that noble, compassionate message? Lafayette, who would not accept his favors and whom he had sought to injure in his son. Not America, but St. Helena, was to be the destination of the man who had crowned and discrowned kings.

Napoleon—Lafayette! The name of one lives with the achievements of selfish glory, and the other with the well-being of mankind. Let us go with Lafayette and his injured son to a different field from this.

CHAPTER XXVI.

THE UNEXPECTED MEETING.

THE arrival of Lafayette in New York, as the guest of the Nation, was the expected event of 1824. He came on the morning of August the 15th, and began what was to him a triumphal march through the repub-lic, whose liberties he had done so much to secure. Banners waved, bells pealed, the air resounded with " Long live Lafayette," and children strewed the streets with flowers. Never, in ancient or modern times, did a reception of any benefactor of humanity more engage the people's hearts.

On the 16th, Lafayette was publicly received in the City of New York. All business was sus-pended on that glorious August day. The morn-ing brought the booming of cannon and the ring-ing of bells. All buildings of importance were gay with flags; the harbor was a canopy of red, white, and blue. Some fifty thousand people crowded the Battery — Castle Garden was a canopy of French and American colors—every-where glowed the motto—" Welcome Lafayette !"

About eleven o'clock in the morning, a steamship bearing the flags of all nations and followed by crowded boats sailed to Staten Island, where Lafayette then was, to escort the hero to the city. He was landed at the Battery about noon, from a steamer bearing only the United States and New York flags.

Seldom in the world has there been felt a nobler thrill of gratitude than that which filled the hearts of the people as that steamer swept up through the shouting harbor. Grand speeches were made on the arrival, and they were followed by reviews, receptions, and illuminations. The city hardly knew any night in those days, when all hearts beat to the one heart of Lafayette.

At one of the brilliant receptions, a young man of chivalrous bearing was presented to the General. He bowed and said :

" You do not remember me. I first met you when a little boy. I have seen you but once since, and then we could not be understood."

" Your name is Huger ? "

" Yes, Francis Kinlock Huger."

"Can it be possible? I first met you when a boy, and you asked me many questions."

"Yes, General, and that was just after you had made your vow by the Carolinian sea that probably decided the fate of America."

"My son, my son! you once offered your life for mine."

"I put myself in peril once for your sake, and for the honor of America."

"My son, my more than friend!" we may suppose Lafayette to have thought. "Do you wish to know what is the most glorious hour of life? It is when one meets an unknown friend who has offered to die for him. What can one say at such an hour? The tongue has no language; poetry fails. The atmosphere of the hero is there. You, you, in the sunset woods near Olmütz, loved me better than your own life. Let me embrace you. This is an hour of which I have dreamed; my heart is full; nothing can express what this meeting is to me!"

In words like these he took the young man to his arms. It is one of the noblest hours of human glory when a patriot meets such a friend.

The accounts of the reception of Lafayette, as

the Nation's guest, would fill volumes, as they have already done ; the noble speeches made by the great orators of the elder day, his own addresses, and the thrilling scenes at Washington, in the South, on the old battlefields, and at the laying of the cornerstone of the monument at Bunker Hill.

These we must pass, but there was one scene at Yorktown that we will wish to review.

It was again October (1824) ; the committee who were to entertain Lafayette at Yorktown met him on the boat that was to convey him thither :

" We are deputed," said the speaker, "by our fellow-citizens, now assembled at Yorktown, to welcome you to Virginia.

" In the numerous assembly now awaiting your arrival, the noblest emotions are swelling in every bosom, engaging every tongue, and beaming from every eye.

" Virginia, of all the States, owes you the greatest debt of gratitude. This State was the chief scene of your services. In the days of her greatest peril Washington selected you, his youthful friend, for the chief command, and to you intrusted the defense of his native State.

"And now, after the lapse of forty-three years, you visit this spot again, happy to renew the recollections of the past."

The beach and the heights of Yorktown were crowded with happy people. All hearts beat faster as the boat bearing Lafayette drew near. The air was a glory of colors, and trembled with cheers.

Noble were the thoughts with which the Governor of Virginia ended his address of welcome :

"No other man, at any date of history, has ever received the tribute of a nation's feelings which have flowed from the heart more gratefully and generously than that you witness now."

At the end of the formal reception a soldier approached Lafayette.

"I was with you at Yorktown," he said. "I entered yonder redoubt at your side." He added— "I was also at the side of the gallant De Kalb, when he fell on the field."

The eyes of Lafayette filled with tears. He must have recalled the vow that the Baron made with him at the Carolinian shore.

Lafayette gazed on the happy faces of the multitude.

This was not the field of Waterloo. It was the field that won a new age for the world. It was the field of a cause, not of men.

The son of Lafayette must here have seen the true greatness of his father's character. What was all they had suffered on a day like this?

CHAPTER XXVII.

LAGRANGE.

IT was at the end of the year 1825 ; Malan, the Jew, had made a journey to Metz, and he left the place for Paris, over the same road he had gone in 1790 with the delegates of the federation, singing :

"It will come; it will come!"

The *Ça ira* still haunted him, and the visions of the 14th of July, when Lafayette laid his sword upon the altar of liberty came back to him. Great changes had taken place. The fall of Napoleon had led to the constitutional throne of another Louis, to be followed by the rise of Louis Philippe, the citizen king, when France was again to have peace. But amid all these changes the principles of the constitution of Lafayette were to remain ; whatever had happened, or might come, Lafayette had enthroned the constitution of the people to be the protector of the rights of the

194

French. To the people of France and of America he had indeed proved the true Knight of Liberty.

"I must visit Lafayette," said the old Jew, as he passed along. "We feel events before they come; our life comes to us first as a dream. I have always wished to meet Lafayette, since I first heard of his name. I have learned that he has taken up the cause of the slaves in the West India Islands and in America; a true Knight, that. I wonder if he ever thought of the Jew.

> " ' *Ça ira, ça ira, ça ira,*
> The humble shall be exalted,
> The exalted shall be abased !'

"Would that there might arise some Lafayette in the world to champion the cause of my people. Did ever any wild beasts treat the beasts of the forests as my own people have been treated by mankind? The liberty of the world can never be achieved until my people have their rights.

> " ' *Ça ira, ça ira, ça ira.*'

"The day will come; the man will come. I am going to Paris, and then I will journey to Lagrange to see Lafayette, and tell him that it was I, the Jew, that sent the bag of gold."

He went to Paris, and dreamed again of that day of liberty, July 14, 1790. He then journeyed toward Lagrange, the home of Lafayette.

Beautiful was Lagrange among the mountains; its streams and its trees. Lafayette had just returned from his visit to America, where he had been the Nation's guest. The whole country, from the Hudson to the Mississippi, had rung with the shout of *"Vive Lafayette!"* His journey, as we have shown, had been a triumphal march under streaming flags and floral arches. All American doors had stood open to him.

It was a féte day at Lagrange as the Jew approached. The children of the country had assembled to honor Lafayette. The Knight of Liberty was beloved by all the people where he lived; these people had often assembled to do him honor, and now the children had come.

Why was Lafayette so beloved by his neighbors, and why had the children assembled to welcome him home from America?

We will let one of his most beloved friends, M. Gates Cloquet, tell the wonderful story of how Lafayette treated his neighbors, who came to love him so greatly. This writer draws the following

Lafayette's wife visits him in prison.

(See page 145.)

picture and we may study it before we follow the Jew :

" To the indigent inhabitants of his canton Lafayette's beneficence was unbounded. Two hundred pounds of bread, baked expressly at the farm for the support of the poor, were distributed to them every Monday, at the chateau ; and in times of scarcity, the weekly distribution was increased to six hundred pounds. The bread thus given was of the same quality as that eaten at Lafayette's own table, and at the seasons last mentioned, each individual received a mess of soup and a sol in addition to his portion. If the poor were seized with some grevious malady, Lafayette visited them, and had them attended to, at his own expense, by Dr. Sautereau, whose talent is equal to his modesty, and whose devotion to the poor sufferers afforded the best proof of his goodness of heart, and his attachment to Lafay-ette's family. There exists at Court Palais a charitable institution founded by the family of Noailles. Lafayette, as having married a Mlle. de Noailles, contributed to defray the expenses of this establishment; and besides, such patients as could not be attended to at their homes were taken care of at his expense at the hospital of Rosay.

" Dr. Sautereau had been an inhabitant of

14

Lagrange for thirty-six years, and was in possession of Lafayette's confidence as a physician, and
of his affection as a friend.   Few have been so
well acquainted with Lafayette's private life as he
was, and few have felt more admiration for his virtues and his noble disposition. 'All Lafayette's
moments at Lagrange,' observed he to me one
day, 'resemble each other, for they are all
marked by good feelings or good actions.'   It
was from him that I obtained the following anec-
dotes, which he related to me with tears in
his eyes, and with the emotion of a man who
regretted that he had himself been unable to per-
form the good actions of which he spoke.

"A man, one day in his presence, spoke ill of
Lafayette, and, by way of answer, he related to
him the following anecdote :

"When Lafayette became possessor of
Lagrange, he wished to make his property as
compact as possible, and with that view purchased
several small pieces of land that had intermingled
with his estate.   One of these small properties
belonged to a peasant named P——, who raised
all the difficulties imaginable, in order to obtain
an exorbitant price for his land ; he was even disposed to go to law with Lafayette about a ditch
which the latter had dug in his neighborhood ; in
short, he took his measures so effectually that he
obtained from the General at least three times the

value of his property. Two or three years afterward, the very same peasant, not content with
having fleeced Lafayette, attempted secretly to
cut some wood in his park; but unfortunately for
him, he fell from the top of an oak, broke his
thigh, and was seized by the keepers, *flagrante
delicto*. Lafayette was informed of the accident
by the wounded man himself, who had been transported to the château, and who applied to him for
assistance. Having learned the circumstances
under which he had broken his thigh, the General
sent Sautereau to the man to set the limb.
When it was observed to him that the individual
whom he assisted was the man who endeavored to
force him into a law-suit, 'No matter,' replied he;
'if I do him good he may feel his injustice to me,
and perhaps regret his exaction on the subject
of our exchange of property.' The case having
proved extremely serious, forty days after the
accident Lafayette had the patient transported to
Paris, and taken care of at his own expense,
though, in reality, the man was wholly unworthy
of his kindness. The fact abundantly proves
that the General could forget base conduct, and
return good for evil.

"In the month of December, 1806, M.
Sautereau was summoned to attend an artisan of
Rosay, named Cerceau, for a fracture of the leg.
The cold was excessive; the poor patient and his

wife, who attended him, had but a small provision
of wood, but they were aware that their doctor
saw patients at Lagrange, and that the excellent
inhabitants of the château were always disposed
to relieve the unfortunate. They accordingly
besought the doctor to make an appeal to Mme.
Lafayette's charity, in order to obtain for them
wherewithal to warm themselves. M. Sautereau
undertook to discharge the commission, and with
the greater readiness, as he was persuaded that
the demand would be favorably received. The
next morning, on paying his visit at Lagrange,
he acquainted Mme. Lafayette with the wants of
his patient, and the necessity of keeping up a fire
night and day in his chamber on account of the
excessive coldness of the weather. Mme. Lafayette, accosting her husband, who was present,
asked if the good people might not be authorized
to take a quarter cord of wood in Lagrange.
'Nay, my love,' he replied, 'give them rather a
half cord, and the poor creatures will then be
spared the trouble of coming so often.' The
advice was followed.

"M. Sautereau made me acquainted with
another trait of Lafayette's humanity and delicacy, which is well worth recording. The wife of
a certain ex-physician of Rosay, who carried on
a trade to enable her husband to live with
respectability, but who had neither the exactness

nor the economy necessary to insure her success in business, had signed a bill payable to order for the sum of four thousand francs, in favor of an individual in Berney, a village near the château of Lagrange. The bill, not having been paid when due, was protested. In the midst of her embarrassments, the poor woman, reckoning upon Lafayette's extreme kindness, entreated him to extricate her from her difficulties, and he, affected by her situation, though suspecting her insolvency, consented to pay the bill. Shortly afterward Lafayette asked M. Sautereau if the lady whom he had obliged was in a condition to repay him according to her promise. M. Sautereau replied that in that part of the country she was said to be ruined; that she was selling her furniture by degrees, but that she was still in possession of some valuable pictures, and that, in his opinion, to accept them would prove the only mode of recovering the sum due from her. 'I prefer losing the money,' replied Lafayette, 'to being paid in that manner, and I am happy to have it in my power to offer as a gift to the poor woman what I had advanced as a loan.' It is necessary to remark that the husband of the lady had never been summoned to Lagrange in his medical capacity; that Lafayette was not even personally acquainted with him, and that, consequently, his generous conduct was not dictated by gratitude, but solely by the desire of doing good.

"At the period of the famine, 1817, the distress at Lagrange was excessive, and all the poor of the country and of the neighboring communes were fed at the château. As many as seven hundred might have been seen there every day. They received economical soup, bread, and money, but unfortunately the purses and the granaries were emptied before the end of the season. Toward the month of June, a family council was held at the château, to take into consideration the means of providing for the wants of so many unfortunate creatures. It was observed to Lafayette that it would be impossible to continue the customary distribution, and that, before the expiration of six weeks, nothing would be left in the chateau.

"'Well,' replied Lafayette, 'there is a very simple mode of solving this problem : we can live in Auvergne; by retiring to Chavanaic, we may abandon to the poor what we should have consumed by remaining at Lagrange; their existence will thus be prolonged till harvest time.' This proposal was joyfully accepted and put into execution by his worthy family.

"During the prevalence of a species of the cholera, which spread havoc in the environs of Lagrange in 1832, Lafayette, in spite of the entreaties of his family, insisted on proceeding to his country seat, to assist the victims of that horri-ble epidemic, in company with Dr. Thierry. The medicine which he took with him, his ice house, a considerable quantity of flannel, linen, woolen blankets, and I may add, his whole house, were entirely at the service of the neighboring villages. 'While the scourge lasted,' said one, 'Lafa-yette was admirably seconded by his son and daughters, Mmes. de Maubourg and de Lasteyrie. M. George and his sisters had summoned to Lagrange M. Cardinal, a young physician remark-able for his zeal and activity. They went together to the villages and houses of the sick, were in movement night and day to assist and console the unfortunate patients, to whom they acted as nurses, and whom they were sometimes obliged to bury, when they fell victims to the disease.

"A boarding-school for young ladies at Court Palais, under the direction of Mme. Ducloselle, had been converted by them into an extensive dis-pensary, where medicine was furnished to all the patients, rich and poor, indiscriminately. The villagers, panic-struck by the rapid spread of the epidemic, and thinking only of themselves, were retreating with precipitation from the scene of desolation, and abandoning the sick; but the arrival of M. George and his sisters revived their

drooping courage. By degrees they grew
ashamed of their weakness, and being convinced,
by the example of their benefactors, that the
cholera was not contagious, they began to follow
them into the houses, and at last consented to
attend to such of their relatives and friends as had
been attacked by the malady. Persons whose
situation enabled them to estimate the expenses
incurred by Lafayette, on the occasion of the epidemic, rated them at 38,000 francs.

"The following fact, simple as it is, will prove
how the inhabitants of the country loved Lafayette. About three weeks ago, I made an excur-
sion to Lagrange, in a cabriolet. By some
fatality I mistook the road, and lost myself toward
nightfall, in the midst of some plowed land.
After a number of fruitless efforts, I almost de-
spaired of regaining the road, when, at a distance,
I perceived a glimmering light. Toward this guid-
ing star I directed my steps, and at last reached
the door of a cottage. An aged female, who was
the inmate of it, was on the point of retiring to
rest, but as soon as she heard of my wish to pro-
ceed to Lagrange, she dressed herself in haste,
put on her sabots, and an old cloak, the numerous
patches of which attested the owner's anxiety to
counteract the ravages of time, and then closed
the door after her, and had the kindness to guide
me, for more than a quarter of a league, through

some most difficult crossroads. As we went along, she talked to me, in her own way, of the loss which the country had sustained in the person of the beneficent Lafayette, and gave me to understand that in acting as my guide she merely discharged a debt of gratitude to his memory. When we separated, the good old woman refused my thanks. I was as much affected by her kindness as I was fortunate in having met with her, since, but for her assistance, I should probably have been obliged to wait for daylight to reach Lagrange, which was more than two leagues distant from her cottage."

Such was the heart of the man, as pictured by an intimate friend, whose château among the hills we now picture the old Jew as approaching.

It was the 10th of October, 1825, on the day before Lafayette had arrived. Nearly the whole population of the canton had met him at the gate. It had been like the arrival of a man at the gate of a paradise ; the atmosphere was filled with the voices of love. It was floral day on the 10th. The little girls of the canton were to assemble in the park and fill the château with flowers.

The same writer thus speaks of this flower day that followed the arrival of Lafayette at La-

grange: "The inhabitants retired only after
having conducted him, by the light of illumination
and the sound of music, under the triumphal arch
bearing an inscription in which they had awarded
to him the title of the people's friend. There he
was again greeted with the expression of the happiness and joy caused to his good neighbors by
his return. During the whole of the next day, the
General was occupied in receiving the young girls,
who brought flowers and sang couplets to him,
and also in meeting the company of the National
Guard of Court Palais, and a deputation from the
town of Rosay. While offering a box of flowers
to their friend, the inhabitants of the commune
addressed him in a simple and affecting speech,
through M. Fricotelle, the head of the deputation;
and no sooner had the oration been pronounced,
than the whole people rushed into the General's
arms, and afterward into those of his son, M.
George Lafayette. On the following Sunday, the
inhabitants of Rosay and the environs offered a
brilliant fête to Lafayette, the expense of which
was defrayed by a general subscription. The
preparations, which occupied several days, were
the work of a portion of the citizens, who refused

the assistance of a single hired laborer. At five o'clock in the evening the apartments and the courts of the château of Lagrange were filled by upward of four thousand persons, many of whom had traveled several leagues to do homage to the man whose name dwelt on every tongue as *the people's friend.*"

It was near nightfall of October 10, 1825, when old Malan entered the Park. The château rose solemn and gray under the long shadows of the mountains; the woods were beginning to wear an autumnal luster, but the park was like fairy land. Children were everywhere, bearing the last bright flowers of the year.

In a tent in the midst of a great meadow, which had been arranged for him, sat Lafayette and his family. The Jew approached the tent.

"It is a happy company that you have about you, Monsieur," said the Jew. "But I see none of my own race among them, and I hope I do not presume?"

"You are a stranger to me, and I assure you that you are welcome. We know no race at a gathering like this, and as for me, I hope that any feeling that esteemed one race more than another has long since died within me. My country is the world, and my race is humanity, and my brethren are mankind. One heart, one brain, one common form, and the same origin and end have all men. The cradle and the coffin bring the first and the final sleep. Whence do you come?"

"From Metz. I am a Hungarian Jew. I have lived in Vienna."

"And what brings you here? Any need of my service?"

"No! yourself."

"I do not remember that I ever did you any service, but I would be glad to remember that I had. Sit down, you must be weary, and I esteem it a compliment that you are interested in myself."

"I once sought to do you a service."

"I am glad to know it. When?"

"When you were a prisoner at Olmütz."

"I am greatly interested. How was that?"

"I sent to you, by young Huger, a little bag of gold. It was given to you on the night of the affair in the wood. You remember?"

"I remember. What is your name?"

"They call me Malan, in Vienna—Malan the Jew."

"I wish that I could have done or could do some service to your race."

"You have rendered services to other races that the common world does not esteem. It is such things as these that have led me to esteem you. General Lafayette, you have the first place in this poor old heart. I know, as few know, the value of liberty."

"Malan, my friend! I would like to talk with you. Let my friend here take you to the château, and give you a more quiet hospitality than you can have here. I will join you there soon."

The old Jew was led to the château.

It was early evening. A rocket shot into the sky. The people were lighting lanterns in the trees, and the hunter's moon, like a gate of heaven, illumined the dusky east. A single star hung over the brow of the mountains, and the woods grew dark in the quiet night. The old Jew was given a liberal meal. Rocket followed rocket on the lawn. The bands began to play, and amid the bright lights of the opening of the fête, Lafayette came stealing away from the field of the festival to meet Malan the Jew.

"You are welcome, more than welcome, as I

said," spoke the Marquis. "I am glad that I owe you a debt of gratitude, though I wish it were the other way. Let me thank you from out of a truly grateful heart for the bag of gold. That it miscarried does not change the prompting and intention of your heart. You spoke to me of young Huger, the Carolinian."

"The young man from the States."

"I met him in America. He was but a child when I first saw him. I was mysteriously attracted to him, perhaps because he had a French name, and he offered his life for me in the affair in the wood, though I scarcely spoke to , him, and did not know him. He came to me amid the noble receptions that were given in my honor in New York.

"Malan, my venerable friend, it is no common event of life to meet one who has offered his life for your sake. My heart melted as he told . me the simple story. He is one of the many sons of my heart. Oh, how rich is life in friends! I bless heaven for them!"

"The world is yours," said Malan. "Napoleon fought for France, but also for ambition and glory. You fought for a cause outside of yourself, and your name will live with the cause. Lafayette, what was it Napoleon used to call Marshal Ney?"

" 'The bravest of the brave.' Ney was a very brave man."

"General Lafayette, he is a braver man who can say no to the field of honor and glory, and to wealth and fame, than he who fights to win what ambition most covets and esteems. You have been able to say no to yourself, in every cause where sacrifice would best serve mankind. In my view, you are the bravest of the brave; and one day the world will so count your name and fame."

" But, my good friend, let me show the picture of one who was as brave as any man who ever lived. See, here is a portrait framed in gold. Let me uncover it."

" Whence does it come?"

" I brought it from America. It was presented to me by the city of Charleston, South Carolina, one of the United States."

Lafayette uncovered the portrait slowly in the dim light.

In the park the fireworks were delighting the

crowds. The moon was rising, and music filled the air.

"This young man," said Lafayette, "surrendered himself to what seemed to him to have been ruin to save me. He was rich, a mere lad, and had a widowed mother. Amid hostile strangers he said in his true heart, 'Welcome any fate, if Lafayette be but saved!' The high quality of gratitude in his heart was more than life. Such a man is a hero. I will transfer the phrase with which you have knighted me to him."

Lafayette set the picture before the light. The Jew started, and his eyes filled with tears.

"That is Francis Huger," he said. "Do you know why he offered all he had for you?"

"Yes, my good friend. Why?"

"What is a knight?"

"A knight? It is he who for honor champions a cause!"

"General Lafayette, you hold Huger to be one of the bravest of the brave. He had a highborn nature, and he looked upon you as the champion of the rights of man—the knight of liberty!

"General Lafayette, a knight makes a knight, and whatever tends to righteousness, that is right.

I shall never see you again. I go out into the night. My days are swifter than a weaver's shuttle. My hard life is glorified in this word of cheer. The thought makes me happy. General Lafayette, I leave with you the voice of time. Knight of Liberty, farewell!

"*Ça ira, ça ira, ça ira,*
The humble shall be exalted!*"

CHAPTER XXVIII.

MAN is not a hero until he can say no to wealth, honors, preferment, or any advantage to himself that he may deem detrimental to the world. Lafayette had indeed said to the agent of the King of Prussia, who had offered him freedom in return for an alliance with a foreign power against his own enemies in France: "No—my name is Lafayette." In that hour he not only said no to a great temptation to gain relief from imprisonment, but what might have been, to another, a great opportunity for revenge.

No man can ever be conquered who has conquered himself. And no man can be a hero, and rise with godlike beauty, who does not make his affections subordinate to his moral will. A man enchained by his affections and passions cannot be free, he is a slave to the earth; all his powers of godlike action are prisoners. The affections are noble under control.

"So many remarks have been made in a party spirit," once said Lafayette, "that it may not be out of place here, to assert that no private affection has ever diverted me from my public duty. In the course of these years of power I encouraged none to speak well of me, and prevented none from speaking ill."

But not only must a true hero be able to say no to any allurement from duty, and rise superior to his private affections, he must be able to lose himself in a cause, and become the soul of the noble principles that he advocates. Such was Lafayette.

"Ah, sir," wrote he from the prison of Magdeburg to M. d'Archenholz, speaking of the necessity in which he had been placed, of exiling himself after the 10th of August, 1792, "how great are my obligations to you for having sympathized with the inexpressible pangs of my soul,—ardent in the cause of humanity, thirsting after glory, tenderly loving my country, my family, my friends,—when after sixteen years' labor I was compelled to tear myself from the happiness of combating in defense of the principles and the opinions for which alone I had lived!"

"Every man," says a great thinker, "is a debtor to his profession." Lafayette recognized that he owed the highest moral character to his position as a leader of the people. He knew the meaning of ruined influence.

When he had not a great call to serve in the national councils or field, he felt it his duty to live as a simple citizen; of this he says:

"'The hope of thus serving my country would be to me an additional motive to preserve undiminished the species of moral power attached to my personal character; and should this hope prove illusive, as it is the only one which I call my own, I have only to balance the individual advantages of fortune or tranquillity with the benefit which the public may still find in my passive state of existence. You thus see that, independently of my natural and insurmountable feelings, I ought, as a matter of calculation, to permit myself no indulgence on this point."

And, to be a true hero, one must seek moral power without the spirit of revenge. It is a mean man that would seek to be revenged on anyone. Lafayette had learned this principle well. One of his most intimate friends and a biographer, after describing his almost boundless charities and his pity for all who were friendless or unfortunate, says : "Lafayette's elevated social position, his fortune, his numerous connections in both hemispheres, enabled him to render important services, and his benevolent solicitude was exerted in favor of distant as well as of nearer objects. He sometimes found grateful hearts, though his kindness was often repaid with the blackest ingratitude ; but it may be said to his credit that he never cherished, I will not say hatred, for that feeling was unworthy of his noble soul, but even the slighest resentment, against a human being. He forgot injuries, or rather, they left no trace on his mind, which was the abode only of kind and generous sentiments. Gratitude was, in his opinion, a feeling which reflected as much honor on the receiver as a kindness on the bestower. Ingratitude he looked upon as the offspring of selfishness or vanity, and he was accustomed to say that with the ungrateful there was no resource ; that the best way was to keep them at a distance when

known, or to avoid them when once made their
victim. Groveling in adversity and insolent in
prosperity, you are everything to the ungrateful
man when he wants you, and nothing to him when
he can dispense with your assistance. Gratitude
is a burden only to a bad heart; for this reason
Lafayette was not afraid of contracting obligations, which he repaid with interest whenever an
opportunity occurred. One grateful heart made
him forget a thousand instances of ingratitude,
and thus he continued to oblige, though his kindness was often thrown away. The happiness
which he felt in doing good would not permit him
to refuse kind offices, and the surest way to oblige
him was to afford him the opportunity of being
useful to others. I have often availed myself of
his kindness on behalf of my friends or of worthy
individuals, and in so doing I felt conscious that I
was guilty of no importunity. His confidence
was, no doubt, often abused, and recommendations
were obtained from him which he would have
refused had he been induced by a little more dis-
trust, or even circumspection, to procure accurate
information as to the objects of his kindness.
Whenever he ascertained that he had been

deceived, he made a resolution to be more reserved for the future; but his natural goodness always got the better of him, and his experience was of but little use in putting him on his guard against fresh solicitations."

He gave himself to the highest cause that commanded his service in early years and he never departed from its principles. Says the same friend of him, in some personal recollections: "Lafayette valued reputation and glory, but cared little for the power that generally results from them. Having one day been asked who, in his opinion, was the greatest man of this age: 'In my idea,' replied he, 'General Washington is the greatest man; for I look upon him as the most virtuous.'

"A short time after a great national movement to make him a king, an Englishman arrived from London to Paris to see Lafayette, and returned as soon as he had accomplished his object. Some of his countrymen wished to detain him, but he refused their solicitations, and said, on leaving them, 'I was desirous of seeing a man who had refused a crown; I have seen him, and return content.'

" Lafayette," says the same writer, " loved truth above all things, and rejected all that could change or corrupt its nature. Like Epaminondas, he would not have suffered himself even in joke to utter the slightest falsehood. He was the mirror of truth, even in the midst of political parties, whose condemnation he pronounced by presenting to them the hideous image of their passions ; he thus offended without convincing them, and the mirror, being declared deceitful, was destined to be broken. I once heard him say, ' The court would have accepted me, had I been an aristocrat, and the Jacobins, had I been a Jacobin, but as I wished to side with neither, both united against me.' "

This is high praise, and it pictures the true way that a young man should enter upon life, if he would have harvests that will satisfy his soul. To follow the Divine Ought that is born in the soul of every man, is to find an exalted contentment in life, joy in death, and the sure elevation to a better existence hereafter.

We have told the story of how once more was the great man's soul to be tried ; how Napoleon Bonaparte flashed forth like a meteor, and gained control of France, and scattered her enemies, and it was proposed to elect him consul for life.

Napoleon knew Lafayette as a true knight of liberty, who drew his sword only for a cause. He sought to draw him after him, and would no doubt been glad to have given to him the place, opportunity, and honors of Murat or Marshal Ney.

Lafayette read Napoleon. He saw that he was fighting not only for the glory of France but for himself and empire. The crisis came. Lafayette was again in the national councils. Should he follow this new star?

Should he vote to make Napoleon consul for life? No!

He voted no. He followed the Divine Ought to his own detriment. He made, as we have shown, Napoleon his enemy, and the conqueror went so far as to cause the son of Lafayette to be ignored in the army.

He saw Marshal Ney come to be called " The Bravest of the Brave." He saw Murat married to the sister of Napoleon and given the crown of Naples. He found himself neglected at the new Imperial court. He had invited it, and he was silent.

But the Ought within him had demanded that vote of NO.

Napoleon brought half of Europe at his feet, and scaled the Alps. The world applauded or shuddered. Would this man possess Europe or fall?

Lafayette could not then be certain, but could be silent.

Had Lafayette, in these dazzling years of the conquests of France, no regret that he had voted no? No! And should Napoleon fall, could Lafayette be magnanimous toward him who sought to ruin even the hopes of his own boy? Yes!

We repeat this experience of the life of Lafayette. *To suffer silence* for the conviction of right and justice is often the noblest achievement of the soul. With all of his glorious deeds in war, there is a great example in this silence of Lafayette.

We here take leave of Lafayette in the simple narrative which we have formed, which has adhered so nearly to history as to have but slight threads of fiction. What is the lesson? Simply this, that character is everything! He was great as the knight that championed

American liberty; great as the creator of the
constitution of France, which, after nearly a century of changes, has ended in one of the fairest
republics on earth; but he was greater when he
said No to self, to luxury, and to every seeming
advantage that could tempt the soul of a man.
He could suffer, and if needs be, die, but he
could not imperil his honor.

"My life and honor both together run;
Take honor from me, and my life is done."

Let us part from this character, whose influence
is immortal, because it stands for a cause, as
Washington parted from him, when he saw him
for the last time.

It was a bright Indian summer day. The roads
of Maryland were glorious with the lusters of
early fall. The air was mellow, and the noon was
past.

They had driven toward Annapolis, Washington and Lafayette. The latter was to embark for
France.

The two generals separated on that day, as
brothers would part whose hearts were one.

But the heart of Washington did not leave
Lafayette. It followed him.

The great life that he had loved grew upon him as he sat down amid the shades of Mount Vernon after that ride. He had not expressed all that his deep nature desired at that hour of parting by the way. So he wrote to this friend what remained to be said:

"In the moment of our separation, upon the road as we traveled, and every hour since, I have felt all that love, respect, and attachment for you with which length of years, close connection, and your merits have inspired me.

"I often asked myself, as our carriages separated, whether this were the last sight I should ever have of you.

"My fears answered Yes.

"I called to mind the days of youth, that they had long fled to return no more; that I was descending the hill I had been fifty-two years in climbing; and, that though I was blessed with a good constitution, I was of a short-lived family, and might soon expect to be entombed in the mansions of my fathers.

"These thoughts darkened the shades and gave gloom to the picture, and, consequently, to the prospect of seeing you again."

If such a life inspired the heart of Washington to such words as these, it may well give the direction of patriotic endeavor to the American youth. Young Huger, in the wood of Olmütz, is a picture out of life, and what he felt, who would not feel, and what he offered, who would not offer, for such as he who rose above self for the welfare of his fellow-men, and was to France the father of constitutional rights, and, to our own nation, the Knight of Liberty!

" *Where liberty dwells, there ever will be the country of Lafayette!* "

THE END.

www.ingramcontent.com/pod-product-compliance
Lightning Source LLC
Chambersburg PA
CBHW030817020726
47499CB00006B/1955